# The Crossing

## Newcastle Poetry Prize
## Anthology 2023

THE UNIVERSITY OF
**NEWCASTLE**
AUSTRALIA

**HUNTER**
**WRITERS**
**CENTRE**

*The Crossing*
Newcastle Poetry Prize Anthology 2023

Hunter Writers' Centre Inc. and the University of Newcastle
Newcastle NSW 2300

Published by
Hunter Writers' Centre inc.
hunterwriterscentre.org


ISBN-978-0-6453756-4-0

Cover image by Leslie Duffin
Cover design by Keighley Bradford
Typesetting by Keighley Bradford
2023 Published by Hunter Writers' Centre Inc.

The 2023 Newcastle Poetry Anthology, *The Crossing*, is
produced primarily on Awabakal country, from work created on
this and other Aboriginal and Torres Strait Islander lands.

Hunter Writers' Centre pays our respect to elders,
past and present, and extends this respect to all
Aboriginal and Torres Strait Islander people.

The birds soar, and the weather soars—
a coming storm against it. How reverent my beloved,
the wind raging in her face, when the kite finds at last
                         the dying light—the ferry pushing
                                        hard into what waits.


                                        ~ Kevin Smith
                                        *The Crossing*
                         Winner 2023 Newcastle Poetry Prize

# Contents

# Introduction

This year, there were over seven hundred poems entered in the Newcastle Poetry Prize. All submissions were considered blind, and we read every one of those poems. It was an arduous but extremely rewarding process. We were advised to each submit an individual long list of one hundred poems to the Hunter Writers' Centre. On the submission of these individual lists, we were provided with each other's lists, which were divided into two groups of poems: those in which there was consensus and those in which there wasn't.

Then the fun began. Meeting in the renovated Catholic church surrounded by bushland which has become John's home on the NSW Southern Tablelands, we spent an entire sunny spring day comparing our choices and working towards a final list. Happily, but not unexpectedly, the poems nominated by both of us were numerous. But we also found there were poems that each of us felt the other had missed, and this meeting gave us the opportunity to argue for poems which had impressed us individually. After much lively and generous debate, we settled on the poems which comprise this anthology. Sadly, though, given the slimness of this volume and the number of excellent submissions, there were many fine poems which did not make the final cut.

We were struck by the high standard of so many entries, but there were traps into which many poems too readily fell. The most prominent of these was too much emphasis on meeting the maximum two-hundred-line limit that was a condition of the competition. Poetry, in its nature, is condensed; there's a reason the poems that affect us most deeply rarely cover more than a couple of pages. Many serious contenders seemed to feel their poems would not be seen as 'weighty' enough unless they approached this maximum length. Consequently, although they had impressive passages, many longer poems did not maintain sufficient intensity or quality. Many could have done with a good edit. In the early stages of his writing career, John recalls sending a multi-paged poem to the inimical Les Murray, and Murray responding, 'Ah, it's a bit long for its length, if you know what I mean.' Yes, Les, we know what you mean.

Many poems seemed to be primarily therapeutic. A good poem can help its maker understand and manage trauma, but the poem itself is often lost when the self becomes its rationale and focus. There's value in restraint, in leaving some tension in the pipeline rather than letting it burst uncontrollably across the page. A good poem engages the reader as part of the process and lets the resonance of well-chosen words do the work. The ability to bring a reader with you into difficult territory, rather than simply demanding sympathy, is one of the hallmarks of good writing. A poem isn't a lecture either, and many of the less successful submissions here seemed to be doing the work of an essay rather than poetry. In our experience, poets rarely know what they want to say until they use the poem to dig into the unfathomable, as Seamus Heaney suggested. Many submissions seemed to be using the poem to express an already formulated concept rather than letting the poem explore something below the mind's surface. Many assumed the 'right thinking' of their makers rather than approaching the poetic experience with tentativeness and humility.

This doesn't imply, however, that good poems are necessarily opaque. We were sometimes disappointed that potentially effective poems were marred by a tendency to be self-consciously obscure; poetry is an inherently difficult art and there's no virtue in making it less approachable than it needs to be. Sometimes the complexity of an experience necessitates a kind of murkiness—Mark O'Flynn's 'D.I.U Eulogy' or Jake Goetz's 'Internal Climates' are good examples of this—but more often than not we felt there was a kind of laziness in the resort to gestures of convolution. The poem on the page is, ultimately, an act of communication. It must be said that, unfortunately, a number of poems appeared to have been AI assisted, or wholly created by AI. It seems that some contributors may have hoped for an Ern Malley moment, where it would be revealed that the winning poem was created by ChatGPT. We'd have enjoyed that moment too—but, at least on the examples we saw, AI is still a pretty terrible poet.

But the poems in this anthology are impressively crafted, demonstrating clear evidence of forensic drafting; they are obviously the result of a process which has been seriously undertaken. The winning poem, Kevin Smith's 'The Crossing' shows a sure command of language and form. In lines spread out across the page like the random rocking of the sea, the poem describes an ocean crossing undertaken by the narrator, his ailing partner, a young girl at the beginning of her life and an old man facing mortality. The crossing in question, then, becomes metaphorical, but the poem never overstates its premise; it is deeply moving due to its gentle restraint, the power of its imagery and the plain but elegant language it employs. The poignancy of its final lines remain with us both.

> The bird soars, and the weather soars—
> a coming storm against it. How reverent my beloved,
> the wind raging in her face, when the kite finds at last
>              the dying light—the ferry pushing
>                  hard into what waits.

Mark Tredinnick's 'Lines for late Winter; Or, the Reef Heron' took second place. This poem also considers mortality, the narrator walking his dog along the seashore while noting the small signs of his body's diminishing. This is a resonant, daring poem, its jagged lines and vivid rhetorical gestures holding a tension between the narrator's sense of entropy and his delight in the physical world. Ultimately, it's the poem itself, the act of its creation, that gives the poem its sense of exhilaration, that keeps the poet from despair. It is beautifully balanced. Tredinnick's poem is not simply another ecstatic example of eco-poetry, it warns as much as it praises. 'Tell yourself,' (it begins,) As a reef of cloud swims in low / Across the estuary, like a contrapuntal tide, / Only that the weather is changing, / And the world is not yet coming / To an end. Tell yourself . . .'

Jo Gardiner's 'A Country Childhood' was third. Despite the innocence of its pastoral title, the poem is searingly anti-Romantic. In grim tercets, it plots the narrator's experience of the savagery of a country childhood, where the slaughter of natural things is both horrific and ordinary, and where a child's complicity in this brutality seems inevitable. The evocative, original imagery of the poem is both confronting and oddly beautiful. As with Smith's and Tredinnick's poems, its strength comes from tension and ambiguity. The craftsmanship of this poem is apparent in every line, the form providing an effective scaffold for otherwise free language. There is nothing complacent about these three poems.

Two poems were highly commended: Dženana Vucic's 'my father sits in a room alone' and Todd Turner's 'On the Vale of Soul-Making'. Vucic's poem uses spare, unadorned language and clipped, blunt sentences to paint an uncompromising portrait of a man scarred by war, a country still bleeding from a decades-old conflict. From the outset, Vucic combines split-second imagery with dramatic enjambment to build collages of increasing intensity. The poem begins, 'A boy drowns in the lake. Another steps on a / landmine. Years before, a man cocks his gun. / My father sits in a room alone. The village is / empty. My father tells a joke. A man hangs himself.' It demonstrates so well how simplicity does not equate to being simplistic.

Turner's poem juxtaposes Keats' loss of his brother Tom and his own slow movement towards an early death with the narrator's loss of his brother. By placing his own experience of death in the context of an iconic one, the universality of human loss is both elevated and made mundane. Descriptions of the landscape are skilful and evocative—evidence of the poet's deep understanding of nature. 'The mangroves link limbs,' he writes, 'and breathe the night's white blaze.' And later 'Green is the colour of the blood in the soil. A buckskin horse,' Turner observes, 'watches with deer-shy eyes.' This is a work of extraordinary imagery.

We wish we could comment on each of the poems in this anthology, all of which impressed us in various ways. When the identity of the writers here was revealed to us, we were delighted to see strong works from familiar names in Australian poetry, but just as pleased to find names we've not come across before. To Chat GPT, we only have this to say: keep trying. Practice makes perfect and it won't be long, no doubt, before you crack a prize like this.

The great value of a competition such as this is in its levelling: no matter what a poet may have previously achieved, all are reduced to only this poem, all are equal in anonymity. When we read these poems, we, as judges, are starting again.

John Foulcher and Judith Nangala Crispin
October 2023

# The Crossing
## Kevin Smith

1

In a café on the top deck, a child takes a step
                    and the floor drops away as the ferry's bow dips
into the sea. She falters,
almost falls; her mother
grips her elbow until her foot
            finds the floor. Twin hulls slice the water open
as we cross the passage, Rachael and I, rocking on
                the ocean's swell, toward the island. The girl, who might not
yet be three, pulls free
of her mother's grip and slaps both hands against
                    a glass wall, demanding the sea's attention.


2


The island rises before us.
Inevitable as time or as stone.
The ferry bucks and dips
            and in the distance masts, like needles,
                    skirr on a wild sea, desperate
to stitch together clouds
            shredded by wind. Beyond the glass, Rachael stands firm
on the ferry's bow
as it ploughs the waves; she takes
             it all in as if this, her first, were her final crossing.
The wind besets her,
and tries to tear away the shawl
            that covers her head, that she pulls tight about a body
              thinned by lingering illness.

3

Her gaze—alert for dolphins,
            for terns and kites—alights on three wet cormorants
slung like drunks on a metal outpost—a marker plumbing the channel's depths.
They hang their wings to dry, but she will not;
                        she watches as they slide past
on the ferry's wake and dissolve
            like history into a grainy spume that blurs the mainland,
the wharves alive with gantry
cranes, container ships—like blocks
of flats—ease up to. She turns to me, her lips
            blue, her eyes tired from contemplating
                        too long what might be inevitable.

4

The girl presses her face against the glass;
            she hungers for salt and air, the stiffening breeze.
She wants the wind, the sea too, the delight in the rise and fall
of a rocking-horse ferry. Her mother
scoops her up and sets her on a seat,
            as if to check a wildness loosening in her; she screams, kicks
her legs in protest. An old man
glares at her with eyes the colour of the sea.
            The girl quietens. He thumps his stick once into the floor
and she stops kicking.
Her mother glances at him
            —a beard stained with nicotine, the smell
                        of fish guts lifting off his coat sleeves.
His eyes turn to the island.

5

Beyond my love, the sky writes
                its fables in endless shades of white and grey,
                                cataloguing every story ever told.
No word of the future, though.
Behind the café counter, a radio spills a sudden flood
                      of inanities across the floor.
If the future's a trick of the mind, it's one
                   I've not mastered yet. Some days
I turn with the tides; most days, I wake on a sea floor beneath a heavy press
of ocean and, like the morning, begin the thing again.
                      I rise now into days that know no horizon.
Some say the future does not exist, but it always did
for me, as if my only belief lay
in all that can't be known
               or seen. My days are silent now. My love's more silent yet.


6

Beyond the windows, a wave explodes and soaks her through. She turns,
her clothes drenched, so too
           the sparse amount of hair she has left.
           The little girl, out of her seat, raps the glass
                   as if to get my love to open the door.
The old man's stare has her stepping back—but still she stands,
eyes on Rachael whose eyes are on a Brahminy kite
           that sweeps low across the shallow sea,
             in shadow now and then in failing light. And suddenly I see
in Rachael—her mind emptied—a moment of forgetting I want time to legislate in stone.
               The bird soars, and the weather soars—
a coming storm against it. How reverent my beloved,
the wind raging in her face, when the kite finds at last
             the dying light—the ferry pushing
                 hard into what waits.

# Lines for Late Winter; Or, the Reef Heron

## Mark Tredinnick

*Tell yourself*
*as it gets cold and gray falls from the air*
*that you will go on*
*walking, hearing*
*the same tune no matter where*
*you find yourself ...*
—Mark Strand, 'Lines for Winter'

Tell yourself
As a reef of cloud swims in low
Across the estuary, like a contrapuntal tide,
Only that the weather is changing,
And the world is not yet coming
To an end. Tell yourself
As you walk with the dog onto the rock platform
And around the point
Into the soft
Artillery fire of first rain
That it's the barometric pressure you feel
In your right hip,
Not yet arthritis, and that's why
Your leg aches a little more sharply
This morning, and tell yourself
That if you are not as nimble among the wrack and volcanic
Intrusions as your young dog,
Among the oysters as the sooty oystercatcher,
Still you are alive and walking upright
And your bones are organ pipes
In which fugues and ancient airs play

And ancestors sing
And your feet among rockpools
Are not unlike your mother's feet all those years
Along the pedalboard,
And that you will go on
Faring your way
A while yet. And as curtains of squall
Close out the horizon, say to yourself softly
That there will be many more curtain
Calls, and as the wind picks up,
And the rain band arrives like its own fanbase,
Remind yourself that
This is a moment of meteorology, a synoptic
Incident; this is not the rest
Of your life. Say again, as if you were swimming the rip upriver,
That the deeper you drop into the end of winter
The closer the start of summer draws,
And that you will go on,
Even though the rain falls hard now
And the dog looks not unlike
The kelp along the strand line;
You will go on, like the reef heron
Making an elegant meal
Of the falling tide. And do not forget
To tell yourself that every song
The chita chita offers
At dawn is not a song of farewell,
And that, like the rain—a mosh pit now—you will set in.
And like the tide, though you fall,
You will rise,

And like the sheoaks, you will inhabit your life
Inordinately,
The way a forest inhabits a tree,
The sky, a bird, the whole world, a moment,
The ocean, a shore.
And your life will be your own life
Utterly, your soul a perfect fit
For your days,
And so it always will have been.

Or so
These late winter lines—a long time coming
Into voice and making land, and spoken here
In sand and wrack and ripple—
So these softspoken lines
Would have you understand.

# A Country Childhood

## Jo Gardiner

Near old Dunkeld bluestones in the faulted Grampians
    where corellas dipped and looped, you stood shoulder
high in scratchy heather and picked blue tinsel lilies,

golden moth orchids and green correas, parrot peas—
    wildflowers with crimped petals studding the ground
in a tumble of splintered stars. But remember, too,

the sweetish stink of flesh gone bad, how wind ruined
    silver banksia, crows gulped steaming guts torn from
inside a rabbit's belly and spilled from beaks as they flew

off, trailing black crinoline. And how a solemn-faced
    child stood in dusky purple leaves below a yellow
wreathe of wattle, a gun held slackly along one arm.

This evening, as you watch the scarlet maple
    bleed out on the lawn, you count them: the time
you fought off dogs hellbent on ripping crimson

chasms in the fox's cloud-soft throat; and returned
    a shallow-mouthed trout from a hook into the brown
liquid soul that was its river; and scared wild ducks

off the lake before the gunmen came, laughter inside
    their slaughter leaking into dawn; and freed a furry
huntsman, long legs unfurled inside a window screen;

and all the bees; and the bogong moth—velvet as cob-
    webs on lips—sifted from water for summer's breath
to dry drenched wings; and countless birds retrieved

from the concussion of windows masquerading as open
    sky; and later, the suicides poised for flight into the blue
you talked back from the edge; and the joey you scooped

from her still-warm mother—her raspy tongue searching
    for touch of kin tasted only your salty skin. She slept
inside a hessian pouch strung from the Aga, the warm

centre of your home, whiplashed by winds funnelled in
    from a southern sea—a skirling coronach for every
creature laid to waste, or left ruined by rifle fire—

like the bird that dropped down dead, when, aged ten,
    you raised the .22, steadied your sights on that knot
of feather and little bones, and cleanly took the shot.

# On the Vale of Soul-Making

## Todd Turner

*To the memory of my brother, Cory*

*Of every ill: the man is yet to come*
*Who hath not journeyed in this native hell.*
—John Keats

I take the long walk home by the river's edge.
The mangroves link limbs
and breathe the night's white blaze.
Fog lifts above the water like the steam
rising from my shoulders. Tonight,
amid a restless breed, with unbroken calm,
I stepped to the swing of a heavy bag,
rehearsed co-ordinates to a slick-screen shadow,
fired the jab: t-tap tap, t-tap tap, like rain
on a windowpane.                     Yet, all the while,
I thought of the young poet and physician,
who, days after the death of his brother, Tom,
coach-clattered over forty miles to watch a prize fight
between two first-rank pugilists, Jack Randall
and Ned Turner. The contest was brutal—
a staggering thirty-four rounds,
two hours and nineteen and a half minutes,
till one man 'broke out with fresh energy'
and the other 'went down covered with blood.'

And what I imagine Keats wanted to see
was how each endured drawn-out pain,
*the feel of not to feel,* as he discovered
in the forlorn wards and at operating tables
of Guy's Hospital, London.

\*\*\*

There are times when suffering feels immaculate—
a pure burning, an invisible flame.
Keats knew all too well of the light
that only the immutable dark can illuminate.
In fact, he courted it, *Darkling I listen...*

So, to delve and disappear with the nightingale?
Or persist with the cinders beyond hope,
through seasons of release
and sweet refusal, willed into assent,
by the winter he had to have?

***

It is spring.
New weather brings new truths, or is it simply
the same hard green ones, riven from purse-lipped
perennials, aired for their second coming,
like the tide-tasselled grasses, which seem to wave
strangely at me, here, on the river's edge,
thirty years on from the day my brother's life ended,
and his new life began.
The one without him.
The one intuited by my mother as the weight
beyond mortal measure, which, by word and note,
attuned the seasons, and set longing straight—
like the gaps between those who share enduring grief.

***

My father calls.
I listen, and breathe
the night's white blaze. *Do you know what
day it is?* he asks,
and as if three decades
dissolves in an instant, he ruminates
the poles of love and loss, and for the first time,

21

<pre>                    tells how he received
the news…
                    I'll never forget the call.
The lady's name was Sister Lynne.
She said, your son was in an accident.
</pre>

*I felt my blood turn blue, you know.*
*Your mother was standing beside me.*
*She caught sight of the slightest of things.*

*I tried to hide it but she saw right through it.*
*Where is he? What time will he be home?*
*There was nothing left to do but ask.*

*So, where is he now? Your son's with me.*
*And, where are you? I'm at the hospital.*
*I'm here in the morgue.*

***

To bear suffering, I willingly reconcile
the day-to-day condition of my being.
I think of it as work, and like to think
of routine reality as play. To play at work,
I devote time to 'a steady upward labour'
and draw on resources of will to sustain me.

To summon the presence, I adopt methods
of pragmatism, then hit repeat.
I imagine the experts call this recovery.
I like to think of it as upkeep, or my morning star.

In this way, I like to rise early,
and sync to the salutes between sun and moon.
Here, I pause for tea and a breather, amid
fire-blown pots where the kindlewood awakes.

Green is the colour of the blood in the soil.
The plant life on my balcony insists.
They seek light from the dark of an abyss.
Theirs is a purified mode of transference.
Mine, I choose silence over shooting the breeze.

***

*Life must be undergone*, wrote Keats,
weeks before he set out on his epic walk
to the Highlands. And before long
he stepped through that vast door
which opened up, proving infinite,
as he began to trek six hundred miles
in forty-three days, Charles Brown in tow.
*Here beginneth my journal*, he wrote
in good-natured self-mockery to Tom,
as if to ease his reality that the maternal
lineage of consumption had re-surfaced,
while staring down a no less new-found
world of their brother George's departure
to America. From here, his first and only
*summer in the clouds*, Keats strode
into his 'living year'. High and low,
he raised the stakes, took everything in,
and arose grounded in his mortal limits.

***

Sunday, my first day off in months.
I am clearing manure out of a yard.
In tin box shade, a buckskin horse

watches with deer-shy eyes.
The air is overrun with heat,
and there's an acre of clarity to be gained.

I drag the fork, then scoop and pile.
This work is doing me good, I think,
as I hack and swathe the ground to its marrow.

It is liberating to give yourself wholly—
*is it not*—and I commit to shovelling dung uphill.
When Keats talked of the 'quiet grave',

he meant, death will be my first sleep,
that here on earth, salvation exists
through discipline. Well, doesn't it?

*Dear Friend,*

*I'm afraid so.*

**Notes:**
'broke out with fresh energy' and 'went down covered with blood' from *Boxiana, or, Sketches of Antient and Modern Pugilism*, Volume 3—by Pierce Egan.
*the feel of not to feel*—'In drear-nighted December' by John Keats.
*Darkling I listen*—'Ode to a Nightingale' by John Keats.
'steady upward labour'—The essay 'Education of the Poet' by Louise Glück.
*Life must be undergone*—John Keats letter to Benjamin Bailey, 10 June, 1818.
*Here beginneth my journal*—John Keats letters to Thomas Keats, 25-27 June, 1818.
'living year'—from *John Keats: The Living Year 21 September 1818 to 21 September 1819*—by Robert Gittings.
*summer in the clouds:* Thomas Keats letter to Miss Mary Ann Jeffrey, 18 May, 1818.

# my father sits in a room alone
### Dženana Vucic

i.
A boy drowns in the lake. Another steps on a
landmine. Years before, a man cocks his gun.
My father sits in a room alone. The village is
empty. My father tells a joke. A man hangs himself.
The punchline is: he hangs himself from a willow.
To understand this you need to know something of
the relative weakness of the wood. Bone will break
it. My father knows. My father is a lumberjack.
Two knee surgeries. Patella, in pieces. A scar like
a bullet hole in his side. Thumb tip cut off and
sewn back on. This is just the beginning. He has
another joke about hanging. The man cannot swim.

ii.
I am tired of bean stew, of cabbage. Peppers in
vinegar. When winter comes, it's in jars. My
father and I do not speak the same language.
I am learning. Prije rata, poslije rata. Before the
war, and after. Before the war I sat in this room.
After, we were gone. Loss is too short a word
for it. Too small. How many letters in twenty-five
years. Some of us are still gone. Some of us,
still. There are no pictures on the wall. Photos
in a pile next to the tv. Papers. Dust bunnies.
Ash. Last year the forests burned. There were
floods. I didn't bring a warm enough coat.

iii.

There's always something to clean. Bathtub
slick with motor oil. Dirt. Small rocks caught
in the drain. Every light switch and door handle
smeared. I buy a new vacuum, new chemicals.
Sweep crumbs out of corners. My father's phone
plays ocean sounds. Shhhhhhhhhh in the night.
My father holds scraps of metal between his
feet, wears sunglasses when he remembers. Welds
jagged edges. Makes shapes. Forgets the sunglasses.
Sparks. Eyes red, weepy. Weeping. His phone on
speaker, max volume. Shhhhhhhhhh. says *sorry can
you repeat the question. Sorry I don't understand.*

iv.

Every night we watch tv. Watch the news.
Watch *Survivor*, Turkish soap operas, sitcoms,
talent shows. My father chain smokes. Fingers
black with oil. Grease. The punchline is: He
wasn't in the attic. He was in the cellar. This
is a joke about April Fool's. On Balkan *Survivor*
one host is silent the entire episode. He only
speaks on the Serb channels. There, our host
is silent. No one stops politics. Flies on fruit.
This year was a bad harvest. Everything comes
from the supermarket. Apples. A watermelon,
guillotined. Brazen peaches, wet and sloping.

v.

There's beer in the dishwasher. Rajika. Juice.
Soda, flat after opening days before. Weeks. Since
I came back my father does not drink. Back, not
home. Not yet. A woman walks a cow down
the street. Long skirt. Headscarf in the peasant
way. Later, a cow lows in a barn behind our house.
It is not the same cow, I don't think. In the war
we had a cow and then our neighbours were
killed and we had two. In the war fifteen people
lived in our house. More passed through it. We
milked the cows. Grew potatoes. Planted mines.
There's one Croat in the village. He comes to hunt.

vi.

I'm sick of not knowing what to say. This isn't a
big house. There's nowhere to go. A wasp flies
in, is lost throwing itself against glass. Thinks
better of it. One day there was a rhinoceros
beetle big as an apricot. Two days in a row I am
stung by bees. I am allergic to wasps, not bees.
My father wants to take me through the dead
orchard to the bend in the river. He wants to throw
sticks for my dog to fetch. He is allergic to tall
grass. Comes home with red welts on his ankles.
His calves. Dark like all the blood's at the surface
waiting to flood out. We need salve.

(after Victoria Chang's *How Much*. The first line 'A boy drowns in the lake. Another
steps on a/ landmine.' directly follows Chang's 'A boy drowns in a lake. Another
opens/his head…'. I have also followed Chang's 12-line stanza structure but the
poems differ significantly in theme)

# Internal Climates

Jake Goetz

he was thinking whether a poem could be as transient
as a drive-thru bottleo, whether the frog playing violin
to wasps in the garden could warm the poem up
he was thinking about the sun, mandarins rotting
in winter grass, about time then, maybe history
ideas he couldn't unpack without excessive amounts
of gesticulations, he was thinking about a blue dragonfly
poised on the leaf of a bonsai fig, about the afternoon
he rode his bike down the alley behind the drive-thru
bottleo in Marrickville, he was thinking about the man
he'd found there tangled in a bike, squirming like a worm
in the sun, he was thinking how the poem stopped to ask
'you alright?', and the man, which the poem noted
was bleeding from his head, simply replied, 'aw mate
donworry, the cops'll pick me up soon', he was thinking
how he helped the man up, offered to call an ambulance
but the man simply got on his bike and rode off
he was thinking how in that poem it was election day
or maybe he was confusing days and it was actually the poem
he'd gone to Jack's and sat in the shade of a tree which
for the love of specificity, we'll say was a jacaranda
he was thinking how warm that day was, the feel of cold beer
in his throat, the migratory history the shade of the jacaranda
evokes, he was thinking about Bolivia, that Swedish traveller
who brewed him coca tea to help his altitude sickness
he was thinking how sprightly he felt walking up and down
the barrios of La Paz, running from dogs foaming at the mouth
he was thinking when he arrived at Jack's he saw a green
and gold swing set, tried to sit down, but his body was too big
so he landed on his arse, spilling beer on himself

he was thinking if the poem were a green and gold swing set
he'd have to say something about the suburbs, something
about scomo and racism, or maybe he'd say something
about two friends from school, how he'd listen to them speak
Lebanese to their mothers when they'd hang out after class
he was thinking how he didn't know they were refugees of a war
that it was perhaps due to this neither had fathers, he was thinking
about his grandma in a London bomb shelter during the blitz
his grandpa across the channel learning the lieder of the Hitlerjugend
he was thinking how they met in 1950s Sydney, how they lived in Newtown
down the road from the Bob Hawke mural that now adorns the side
of the Carlisle, he was thinking about his own father, about the years
he stopped working at the refinery to start a mowing business
he was thinking about the smell of Saturdays, freshly cut grass
raking leaves for pocket money, an old woman feeding him stale biscuits
from an old Arnott's tin, *wallah*, that word he'd learned from Ali
he was thinking how it translates as 'swear to god', and how
in year 3 or 4 or 5 or 6 Ali had said 'swear to god miss, it wasn't me'
and Mrs. Sharpe had sent him out, yelling 'you will not take
my lord's name in vain!', he was thinking whether a poem
were a type of God in the sense that everything is a thought
caught in an un-ending web of dialogical sensation, he was thinking
how every web is a poem and how every poem is a planet
forever coming to terms with changes in its own internal climate
he was thinking how the sustained indeterminacy of a poem
perpetually thinking might convey a sense of liminality
in which he could finally feel at home, he was thinking
that if someone said this poem was post-modern he'd call them
post-wanker and that'd be the end of it, he was thinking
that probably wasn't an insult but the fact he cursed showed
he felt vulnerable and perhaps then it said something about his youth
he was thinking about what it meant to write a poem as transient
as a drive-thru bottleo, as if each word were a coat wrapped around

the body of a sentence that could never completely undress
he was thinking whether *transient* was the right word, whether
he should look it up or right-click 'synonym' (*fleeting, passing, brief,
temporary*), he was thinking that the poem, owing to its length
was hardly brief, but could be if it were read as a type of star
a flicker of light in the greater expanse of the cosmos, he was thinking
how stars and the cosmos are cliché, but perhaps it was better
than pouring concrete into the Milky Way, he was thinking
how he worked in a bottleo after finishing school, how he routinely
racked packets of ciggies, he was thinking about that work meeting
when the manager clicked the shits, noting 30 packets were missing
he was thinking how all five workers had been doing the same thing
and so instead of being fired they simply paid for what they had taken
he was thinking how understanding the manager was, or perhaps
frightened, for he also doubled as their drug dealer, he was thinking
that 'bottleo' said something about himself, if not his uncle
who drank himself to death, he was thinking about an artbook
by Ed Ruscha, 21 BOTTLEOS, the first project in his down-under
photo series, he was thinking about North American petrol stations
the way the world would never change because it would never stop
changing, he was thinking of Charles Olson, how tall he was
how if he'd ever met him he probably would've said something half-
stupid, half-smart arse, like 'you ever been to Tasmania?'
he was thinking how simple Australians are, how refined
in their simplicities, he was thinking he'd never stopped attacking
his own country, how that country didn't exist, so maybe he was just
attacking himself, he was thinking how the poem might get it all wrong
and that it's a Sunday so he should probably just go for a walk
he was thinking that if the poem closed its eyes it could hear
tennis balls being hit, muffled voices in the wind, a freight train
heading south-west, then lorikeets speaking between trees
like rustling keys in a pocket of air

# A Garden of the World

Jean Kent

*1. My Mother at her Funeral*

Looking absurdly alive in a photo, back-lit,
you welcome us with an out-in-the-bush smile
under a wide hat, and a swathe of kurrajong leaves.

In the middle of a COVID lockdown, like you
almost everyone who attends has become virtual.
Your family tree, so precise on paper, now is ghostly,

its arms like the tangle of your garden by moonlight
holding the distant faces of sisters, nieces and nephews,
wan as sleeping birds at four a.m.

Long before your death, when you were wondering
what you'd be remembered for, I asked you
what you were proudest of from your life.

I expected you to say your garden, or your plantation—
this world of leaves you grew from nothing—
but with unexpected diplomacy and kindness

you said it was your children—these other gangly growths
which couldn't always flourish. When the slideshow of your life
switches off, your children will plant most of your ashes

as you wished, boxed into the last corner
of your family plot. The rest of you we will take back
to your garden, and your plantation, to scatter

light as breath over your always welcoming earth.

*2. Her Always Welcoming Earth*

Ahead of your time, you cultivated a multinational garden.
All cultures were welcome. Roses from China,
tulips from Turkey, hibiscuses and hebe,
diosma's 'Breath of Heaven'.

On your scrap of land the nearby city hadn't claimed, yet,
the camphor laurels and the wattles walled us in,
their natural co-existence of leaves and light
in easy harmony round our house.

You knew your plants by botanical names. Cherished
them like children. And always could find space
for one more. There were no hysterectomies
on your eight acres. Graves, yes—

but every gardener must be philosophical, know loss
and follow the slide of the spade with a plant.
It would never have been possible to recreate
your own growing place—

no ridges or endless views to horizons under suburban sky—
but still you rewrote your own life story
with wonga wonga and pennyroyal, eucalypts,
macadamias and Bunya pines.

Wherever your curious feet took you, you gathered seeds,
reaching up past dying whisker-white flowers
to gum nuts, or black bean pods' stilled boats—
until all those other

acres of earth you had walked on were remembered
in this haven, this plantation of impossible hope
and cautious co-existence, where the sky

sang over you,
and always, there were birds.

*3. Always, there were Birds*

Last days. Nearly a century on this earth. Some mornings now
you sun-soak on the back landing, the door
to your kitchen open—that black space
where a blue tongue wanders—

where, earlier, with dew and red volcanic soil on your slippers,
you unrolled the *Chronicle* from its prison
of tight plastic, ironed the pages flat
with your teapot

then checked for funerals for the few friends you've not yet
outlived. The black newsprint is a blur, a daze
you can't read after staring out from under
the frangipani and the native jasmine

to your garden in its white-out of sun. A butcher bird,
mock innocent in the falling leaves makes its own
too-sweet melody, and currawongs in the dizzy
camphor laurels ask 'Why?'—

'*Pourquoi? Pourquoi?*' was your translation of their call,
that echo in the background, quite often,
when we talked across our own
distances, by phone.

A crow has dropped torn bread from another home
into the birdbath near the lavender.
Bowerbirds will come later, to dance,
scold one another and drink.

For now, in this bower of your last days, you are as close
as they are to the sky, the leaves, the earth.
You are a wren, almost lost, content.
The garden of the world is yours.

# Bukovina

## Christopher (Kit) Kelen

*a little star still falling*
*even as we speak*


**night train to Vatra Dornei**

so much of it is village dimly
coup upon coup
cropping through flat lands

hear only the speech of steel wheels
track clatter and rattle, all to the north

towers of old smoke until the mountains come

passing away like a country, the night
the place that was before

in through an open window, it is a headlong thing

the Romans laid these Dacia lines
this must be the thousand year train

undoze for first light
that's how long we've been

fine cloud, coarse
barns to fill, hummocks ring

peach, birch, pine

a mess of wires, cranes, river runs
all the industrial trackside leavings

and from some windows
clothes hung to freeze

churchyards full of the gone
old car wrecks cast to the sidings

the stolid station master with the flag
now all the flush tints come

mist yet here there too

the valley opening, opening
sometimes whole farms dance

the green all greener than the hill is high

fences and tracks leading where

tin tile timber roof
crosses all round

old walls and yellow wells
the road itself runs by

snow pockets the furthest view

**I love a fence falling**

gone off its way

left languish, nor by wire now touched

perhaps its others are taken for smoke
scratches of pencil on paper

perhaps sunk far in time

just a post stood
where the rust once fell

sculpt first
some rings of a tree
for a while

can you call it such?

it's for the ants to carry away
it's for the worm

pure as rot

in the end
this map in the head is lost

and still such a place
will be somebody's home

this too is a sort of soil

**all that we touch**
*poem at Câmplung*

even in the snow, our leavings

once fruit fell at our feet

an axe through the head of the forest
a cross saw, the body in half

that was us and is

the winecart comes
a moment's joy

ladder—timber as clouds are

the lowing fields of dung

all our own work

he and he—all that was done

and she, like a shame indoors
ladling smoke, sadly gone

we make our iron tracks through the green
bare limbs, call ourselves winter

the house is a head
it won't matter
how fast, how slow

who has sense would tremble

## cuckoo

bit of a cuckoo high in the hills

just one note short of the koel
but this one invented the clock

we all repeat the childhood against us

we were never on time
how can we agree?

you can't argue with the cuckoo

unlike the woodpecker
it vanishes without a sign

I wouldn't call it singing, would you?

though, like your parents, it remains to scold
just a bit further off
a now-and-then hesitation perhaps, for emphasis

it won't let up
not a pause in which to reply

you have the boots and the heart for this
you have to climb higher is all

**they decided to dig up the whole town**

someone must have been elected, appointed
had to have thought of it

roads and pavements, sewer mains, all the supplies
every street, the roads out of town

graveyards! the dead went free …
many of them joined in digging

no one could remember what they were looking for
there was a kind of stubbornness
characteristic, some might have said

hi-vis vests and ten o-clock shadows
they dig as they shout as they
have their own language for this

they dig in the shade, dig in the sun

how the machinery roars!
rusting down through generations

so that was how it went

when they finished with the town
they started digging up mountains
they had to take out the forest first

soon they will start on the sky

## the bells are still ringing

the bells are ringing
they won't ever stop

not everyone believes yet
not everyone attends

these are the bells were sent to save us

dogs go berserk, driven mad by

bells go on regardless
so loud! no one's ever heard themselves think

a bird in the bell must be brief, no nesting

here's a kind of universal tinnitus
heathens beware!

many have wished on them
or called a curse and hallowed be

some say it's a Sunday thing
but the bells are everywhere

for sanctification, bells ring themselves silly
there can be no argument with bells

a kind of joy to bend the neck
to make obeisance

a king inclines to ring them too

all night the bells toll out, bats flee
vampires do their dark

bells drown all the singing
what muezzin could survive?

bells are tolling up crusade
bells ring for an *auto da fé*
and for thee

a wedding, a baptism, funeral, crowning
the destiny of dynasties
all these things are to unravel
the bells have spelled disgrace

even carillon
was never quite what you'd call a tune

bells are well before time, they are after

someone has to have been swinging from the rope

and like the cuckoo in the clock
they make the world machine

should they ever stop
and I know they won't
those bells would still be in my ears

who forged them?
and who hung them where
all the town would have to hear?

these are things must not be asked

where is the well known dragonfly?
but fast asleep elsewhere

**peasants on a train**

go west
and past the rapeseed fields, fresh ploughed

have the smell of work that can't be finished

there is this cloud of a hilltop passed
always the sun in the eyes

little smoke machines
out on the road
they go the other way
to a future

and these less-than-washed
tender they are for their own

they are building an extra storey on the old farmhouse
and maybe one higher after that

stork on the nest like a statue of height
it all depends on the neighbours

this Christ on the cross is theirs

**untitled**

just as dollars so a roof
so the shirt on my back

thus I put up a store
could call it antsworth
a squirreling

and lifework
all these little proofs against time
the tussle with urges

lay down in the sun and the snow
nothing there that bites but sleep

be eaten next spring
in the first thaw
fresh as the day you were born

# Inheritance

## Eileen Chong

Sifting through the remnants of what was left unsold,
my mother uncovers three steel cooking implements:

two ladles (one larger, the other shallower) and a wide,
splayed spatula. Their bodies are burnished gunmetal;

their wooden handles have been worn smooth.
They gleam with the patina of heat and daily use.

There is but a single photograph of our hawker stall.
My grandfather, his dark hair raked back, poses

in the foreground. Spoons laden with sambal and narrow wedges
of lime line the front counter. Yellow and white noodles nest

behind glass, next to eggs stacked high on cardboard trays.
The immense wok; the roaring flame. Plumes of smoke—

Where is my grandmother? The tools of her trade now lie
unmoving in a box. Her smile grows still in a shadowed frame.

Once, in her kitchen, her grandchildren crowded around
the stove, watching. No one had thought to take notes.

She minced garlic with a cleaver, and in one smooth
movement, scooped and tossed its contents into scalding oil.

How the garlic would sizzle. The aroma of its browning.
Eggs cracked and beaten in the pan, handfuls of noodles

eased from a tangled mass. Shelled prawns (heads and tails
left on) and a ladled measure of stock. She scraped at iron

with the spatula, crisping the ingredients, mixing them in, then
rapped hard, thrice, on the edge of the wok. Sparks would fly.

Next, the plates: each piled with steaming fried prawn noodles
thick with gravy, complex with spice, and sharpened by citrus.

No record but in these tools. This hunger: my only inheritance.
I raise my chopsticks, lift the noodles to my lips, and I feast.

# Illustrated Odes to the Forty Scenes of the Garden of Perfect Brightness

## Jo Gardiner

*In1860, during the Opium Wars, British and French troops destroyed the vast garden of the Qing dynasty.*

Well, what is it that you want? they asked Dupin,
the French trooper, when it was all over.

*I wish to be faithful to the facts of what
happened, of what is there.*

But there is 'no there, there.'
*Then I will be faithful to what is not there.*

Afterwards, Dupin stood there in the Summer
Palace, the moon and sun both bloody red now—
not with fire, but with its lazy drift smoke wound
in seams of light once

　　　　　teased and amazed by bees
and exotic birds that trailed their golden scarves
through morning's tide. Now, it is only the crows
that climb the Fragrant Hills and troll deep inside

a windless, blackened space in search of elm trees
with shadows woven thick with forest honey.
From this ancient place, the Qing had drawn virtue,
from the artistry now

　　　　　not there—the gardens,
their pavilions and sunlit rooms, all burnt.
Here, avenues of green willows saw peasants
in straw shoes drop to earth in awe, and humble

秦

servitude swept the path before Qianlong, son
of heaven. A loved scholar—his nose always
inside a book—and descendent of the Qing,
he wore his moral

秦

                    wisdom cinched as lightly
as his sash, inviting foreign tongues, beliefs
and different gods to his kingdom. This fulcrum
of the wheeling world perused his concoction:

秦

grand palaces in baroque and rococo
for his people. He built a stupa to house
his mother's hair and a bridge of bianco
marble with veins as

秦

                    pale as the silken throat
of his favourite empress, Xiaoxian. Qianlong lay
on her feathered bed and ate a roasted thrush,
smiled—with whisky-coloured eyes—at some *cocasse*

秦

they swapped as he drank her smoky tea. Moonlight
brushed a palace in the trees and, at his touch,
her plumage rustled secrets inside wings spun
from spinnerets in

秦

                    filaments. Her lightly
perfumed hair flowed long and low over Qianlong's
shoulder, and in an encounter—that may or
may not have even taken place—their bodies

秦

crossed the night's border. The winter Xiaoxian died
fell harsh, and it saw Qianlong unhinged—a door
blown wide and banging in wind unattended.
Snow, like incense ash,

47

               settled soft on her grave
and not for a minute did cold release him
from the sky's blue edge. Beyond his Sitting Rocks
and Winding Stream, the pond lay like a frozen

moon: a blue wind scrawled leaves across its frosted
face like ill tidings on a letter's page. By
the arched gate in the bamboo grove, the iris
waited, tremulous

               beneath the ice, the air
sharp as glass, and every breath knifed his grieving
heart. Spring, when it came, favoured the growth of lush
woodland, and purple parrots, their long tails flared

in crimped and tightly pleated crepe, cavorted
through Qianlong's forty scenes of Perfect Brightness—
from the garden of Eternal Spring, across
the Peony Terrace

               of the Engraved Moon
and Unfolding Clouds and beyond the camber
of hills. Inside folding gates, a garden not
seen outside a dream: peonies blushing pink

at their own opulence. Mazes. Gazebos.
Like blossoms, ideas blew through open windows
where Qianlong studied symmetries in music,
and scored palaces—

               as if to silence grief—
from purloined western pictures he saw. Restless,
he paced all his kingdoms: from Manchuria,
he brought tree jackals and leopards to mingle

with his tigers, wolves, and badgers. And from far
away, like a prize won, the rare Tibetan

golden gazelle—the chiru—loved for her soft
shahtoosh. He planted
秦
oaks, camphor trees, green pear,
and date plum. For his lakes, he brought home water
scallion, white-lipped flower lilies and knot-
weed. Stroke after bravura stroke, the garden
秦
found its realm. Each day at dusk he prowled a path
from pagoda to pagoda, past summer-
houses, cloud-shingled temples, and carillons
in rhyming chains of
秦
chimes down to Xiaoxian's grove
of orange trees. Above, he watched cloud shadows
driven by the breeze and, streaming like dark hair
strewn on a pillow, travel the grassy hill
秦
and—as life does—change form from one fleet moment
to the next. And it was inside these gardens
a century later—when French and British
troops arrived—that
秦
Dupin stood like a flower
astonished at the light. Within eight hundred
acres stood the Emperor's Private Palace,
and The Princes' School, his Deep Vault of Heaven,
秦
full of art and writings from the past: Qianlong's
library lined with works of generations.
At his desk of lilac wood, he sat and took
his empire's measure,
秦
and walked the poems he wrote
into books he slipped inside boxes, and changed
the whole world with wise words he sent far abroad—
each page stamped with his nephrite seal. But Qianlong

was long gone when, jealous its splendour just might
rival grand Versailles, the French believed it theirs
to squander, and finding solace in reproach,
looted jewellery of

                        rose stone and orbed jade,
milky quartz and prase, and amber orpiment,
heaps of crepe, and cloisonné. They bowled the great
vases at mirrors that fell to polished floors

in a million broken chords. As Qianlong's rooms
and gardens beat with drums and the conches crowed,
the British, with stones and rocks instead of hearts,
ran amok and torched

                        the lot. The acrid smell
of melted stealth glowed at the horizon's edge,
and the Luminous Temple fell to its knees
in worship of its name. The scent of smoke came

in search through white birches, and the gazelle felt
her nose quiver. In her liquid eye, gardens
quickly burned, a scarlet and wounded sky writhed
with blinded birds,

                        the fish all boiled in the ponds,
and the dragon lost its many silvered scales.
The bells sank deep beneath the waves, open-mouthed
and drowning. Like hot breath on glass, the ashen

face of Qianlong appeared in the fire's blue
unflinching stare. Eyes lit with agitation,
he watched the firestorm squall across the hills,
and saw darkness shroud

                        the truth, whole dynasties

of noble stars already dead. The vandals,
now drunk on crimson, danced their fire-polished
faces into stupor, ripped leaves from ancient

秦

books where respect lay fallen in the gutters,
and dipped the paper rags in fire to light
their pipes. Hidden behind locked and bolted doors,
three hundred eunuchs

秦

and trembling palace maids—
polishing the silver to quell their terror—
burned to bony husks and left their brief shadows
in the air. In the library, Dupin snatched

秦

from its red and lacquered box, Qianlong's huge book
of illustrated odes and kept it safely.
A dream dismantled, the British raised their flag:
don't ever mess

秦

with us again. This garden,
Dupin wondered, does it have an afterlife?
Now, only stony stubble grows in fields where
pigeons gather; Qianlong's garden of Perfect

秦

Brightness waits in a Paris bibliothèque.
Like small flame heads flaring in the dark or pass-
words to portals, the steady brush strokes—all switch-
backs and slender tails

秦

like waving stems of grass—
overthrow plunder: in turning, pages build
their temple to the odes, and exhale what's still
there—the orange scent of Xiaoxian's fallen hair.

This poem was sparked by reading about the *Illustrated Odes to the Forty Scenes of the Garden of Perfect Brightness* in 'The Looting of Yuanming and the Translation of Chinese Art in Europe,' Greg M. Thomas in *Nineteenth-century Art Worldwide—A journal of nineteenth-century visual culture* Vol. 7, Issue 2, Autumn, 2008.

# Bird, Grieving

## Roberta Lowing

### December

I walk through the hospital grounds    follow the road down
past windowless white-washed buildings      heat-eaten lawn
Next door    the world that is leaving    floral curtains
on a brick bungalow    swimsuits and beach towels hanging from
the old Hills Hoist    wet corners draped over
a red plastic swing set

I walk on    There are no trees here    just a few scrubby bushes
beside a bleached-grey timber fence    the quivers and prickles
of birds and other creatures have retreated into
the cool calm forest where gums grow a hundred feet

Today there is movement beside the bitumen
        two white-winged slender-beaked
        sentry heads swivel to watch me
        a small white fuzz-ball on whirring toothpicks
runs from the corner of my eye across
the shrivelled grass    into the nearest bush
whirring and cheeping

The heron parents stretch their necks
the black glass of their eyes follows me
asking        *How did we come to be here?*
or more likely    *Why don't you all go away?*

One more patch of arid grass to the rehabilitation centre
with its security guards and check-in desk    laser thermometer
stopwatch re-set for the daily solo visit
the usual plus-one family member tearfully
pleading on the concrete porch

Along the corridor of too many trapped smells
        bleach and urine
        the least of them
past open bedroom doors
past silhouettes slouched in chairs or sprawled on beds
eyes wide at the ceiling
everyone waiting for peace of mind to arrive
like that letter long-delayed from a place without anxiety

An hour with my father then out again
dragging bags of dirty washing    paperwork
        uneaten plum pudding
If mood were sky it would be winter
but it's a Christmas day so bright
the darkest sunglasses are no barrier against the light


        The next day and the next
the heron chick flees through the cracking leaves
        gasping and open-beaked
chasing its cheeps and squeaks
already knowing it must swallow every tell-tale sound
        muffle every loose note of distress
        silence every protest at the inexorable
        unjust work
        of living

The day after
the grass is empty although
is that a clot of white spread beside the sun-struck fence?


        By New Year's Eve the clot is gone
but the heron parents patrol the faded palings



        *There were two chicks before* says the gardener
*but the first one went a few weeks ago*
        *A cat got it or the python everyone reckons*
*lives in the hospital drains*
Maybe
I say   the parents hid
        the second baby
        she's tucked up somewhere
*Little legs couldn't run fast enough*
says the gardener

        The bushes are silent
and the leaves
the heron parents step this way
and that
they pivot and retreat on unsteady limbs
They turn their glassy eyes to the fence
bend to the gouges in the dirt

        Why stay here?
        Why not go
        after the first one died?

53

~~~

## January

The Capitol is stormed        The English enter
another lockdown and Germany Italy France
China    the Philippines    and us again and again

Politicians the world over are
smarmy smirking or uncertain
The royals are squabbling
another bad omen for un-royal families divided
by new fractures
        *People are getting weirder*
says the friend forced to work the plague months
on the customer service frontline

I carry more paperwork
down the glistened road
heels sinking into the melted bitumen

I lean sideways
under the weight of the word
        *Why*
                *Why*

Why us
when all we ever wanted
was to lie beneath cool trees
and sleep unconcerned

        My father is still blinded after his operation
shouting at nurses to close his bedroom door
        His ears twinge at every stranger's voice

        even my words have too many syllables
Conversations about washing    paperwork    medication
are dead-ended by
        *If you don't want me*
        *to visit any more ....*

The knock-out punch to once-kinder
ways of talking

Outside with washing and paperwork
        The bird parents sway beside the fence
eyes vacant as dust

I say to them
        Why are you tethered
        to this place of grief?
        You want to go
        You must go

Why don't you cry?

*Cry damn you*

Cry black tears red tears white tears tears of rage tears of shame
Cry snotty snuffly swollen-nosed tears tears that burn like acid
tears that melt titanium tears as long as night tears unstoppable tears
irredeemable tears irreversible unbelievable inconceivable a year ago


~~~


## February

Lockdown shenanigans turn legal
mail is missing     bank statements
rights are ignored
*What the hell is a fungal mouth infection?*

Summer grinds away
the borders whiten with heat
the grass crackles

        Somewhere a snake hisses

At my mother's nursing home
the staff are careless harried sneering worried
overworked under-numbered     contemptuous of families
who don't keep their elders close

Clients who arrive upright and bright-eyed
reduce to frail inmates laid back in their padded chairs
        *(We call it the Chair Of Death*
        says the medical equipment rep
        *Once you get into it you never*
        *get out)*

All day the inmates drowse in God's waiting room
    Curled like sea horses on their sides
they stare at the ceiling unconcerned
no longer thinking *How did we get to this place?*

On television sets welded to high corners
violence flows and ebbs and flows

Arguments about paperwork   permission   missing money
hiss beneath television static
*Why aren't we leaving this place?*

Separations irreparable

    My mother's new nursing home
turns out to be much like the old but more expensive
New nurses    same government forms
same lies in the case notes    falls bruises hungers
skipping across work-shifts   small hard pebbles
skimming cess-pools
to lodge in the husband's weeping eye

Any questioning recorded as
medical interference   Any replies coil and tighten

More paperwork
at the lawyers'

    Why do you stay
I say to the heron parents

    You've done more than enough
    You can't save anyone's life
    You're pointlessly tethered
    to this place of grief

You want to go
    You must go


Go

~~~

## March

Walking down to my father
with clean washing      new paperwork

The heron parents are by the fence
necks curled gracefully as a white fledgling
feathered now not fluffy
runs on long spindly legs out from the bushes
a worm in its beak

    *Oh the relief*

Give us this sign
and another and another

    *Any sign*
    *of one good thing*

The foiling of the python
the drying of tears
by calm cool trees
the eating of a worm
unconcerned.

# Convergence
## Jo Ward

A confused wind is tossing itself
about the café, troubling patrons;
someone next to us has just lost a cup.
I can hear the elderly woman behind me
is very upset, and trying not to be,
about ideas of God—of what is holy—
changing. She is resigned, at turns,
bristling. Cold then warm. I catch
something about convergence and
a (controversial?) fourth awakening.
I smile, a little sadly, at my son
who sits opposite: feet dangling
from a high-chair, picking his muffin
apart. My own evangelism evaporated
long ago: I listen intently (secretly
wondering what she means by the word
convergence). It is blowing a gale
through the café now. People are trying
to get warm: hugging themselves,
rubbing their legs like kindling. One woman leaps
up from her chair to seize a fugitive
menu. I shiver and reach down into the chaos
of the nappy bag, fumbling for a jumper
when I feel that familiar tug—tug—tug
at my sleeve: a little brow, furrowing: a face
so particular. It is each day changed
before my eyes: the world, an altar grows
diffuse—expansive—suddenly, as air.

# The Weight of a Marriage

Audrey Molloy

*i.*

There once was a woman who cut her foot
      clean off, just to be free
of the jangling charm anklet
she'd fastened to herself, dragging around
its heavy little kettle and cutlery set.
The racket when she turned in her sleep!

She gets about these days on stilts
with rubber tips and no one notices
her missing foot. They look up to her,
shading their eyes with rolled-up hands.
*It might be painful up here,*
      *but it's so quiet.*

*ii.*

When she first put it on, the marriage felt loose,
a cotton nightdress she'd have to grow into.
She filled her days with busyness, arranging
the severed heads of camellia stems in crystal bowls,
learning how to make fiddly things—filo pastry,
and babies, which are even more complicated.

She carries a glass of milk across the room,
treads carefully, catches sight of herself in the glass—
      she looks like an angel—tilts
her chin a hair's breadth. The gravity of it:
milk running down her arm
onto her hem and the pretty rug.

*iii.*

She learned that you could keep it light with tricks:
      line-drying linens in full sun, neatly folding in
the warmth, and, instead of kissing deep, on the mouth,
you could air kiss, the kind of kiss that's not a kiss at all—
small engraver of nothing, just another kind of weather,
or a bellwether for the end of something.

A husband's not the only kind to keep a lover
in his arms, another warming on the back boiler
      until a swap can be finagled.
There's a rat in the thin space between
a tree and wall, where a girl will crawl
on a quilt of brown pine needles.

*iv.*

There once was a man in a low armchair,
who leant over a dismembered newspaper
with all the concentration of a nerve surgeon,
doing the important work of men,
keeping abreast of all the important things
      going on outside in the world.

      And a woman at a piano,
picking out a tune, pencilling in the notes
she's forgotten how to read. Her husband
rests his hands lightly on her shoulders
as he passes. She does not look up
but the notes she plays are full of tenderness.

*v.*

When they burst in and slit him open,
they found his wife, stone dead, coiled
in the core of him like a gizzard stone,
diminished, but perfectly formed
from ring-finger to rubber glove.
And there were softened bones of wives of other men,

and other women who were the wives of no one.
A heart can bruise like a fruit.
What do you call that colour again,
since you don't have *aubergine*?
Ah, yes, eggplant. Choose carefully:
pick one that feels heavy for its size.

# A Country Postman

## Andrew Heath

Ploughman's Rise takes its toll on burnished north wind days
that torment his hip with every pedal push against the wheel,
gouging rutted tracks that crisply jangle turning spokes—
pausing at the flowering gum, nestled into the smooth contour
of the crest of the hill; alighting unsteadily,
he stamps his foot firmly against the cramp, tension easing
from muscles and skin, receding from his mind, too,
in the solitude of speechless plain below;
unhurriedly sipping spring water from his old canteen,
he sits against the trunk, breathing deeply,
watching rowdy spinifex pirouetting down laneways that
net the undulating landscape more comprehensively than
sacred oaths; here, sometimes, the ghosts of past days
are exhumed from a faultless memory that will not deny
the existence of pain, futility, and the ceasing of care—
the reality laid skeletal, bare—leave nerve-endings raw and harsh;
clam weeping eyes shut against the grainy flare of despair.

Joining the fanfare, a patriot, the gaudy aroma of optimism
filling his lungs—the solitary youth wasted little time
taking up his gun, marching down complacent streets
draped with bunting peopled by faces imagining a carnival reality,
the ocean still opalescent in the blushing heat of late spring;
took, ahead of his time, the mantle of man—leading from the front—
first out of the boat, thrusting himself into sea amid plumes of spray—
then first shot, thudding back with the sudden impact
against the landing craft, hip shattered, shrapnel slicing his scalp to the bone,
burned and thrust back aboard in the carnage of boiling air;
firing wildly into the sky through oily fumes until his magazine was spent,
idly observing the spent cartridges swimming along the deck
mixing with his own blood, then letting his rifle slump next to him,
until he was hauled to safety and unconsciousness.

His war was over—first to hospital, too—cut and bound into submission,
infection burning him more than bullets, stealing his resolve
until he nearly gave up, slowly clawing back in stubborn resistance,
to some measure of health as days blended unsteadily into years,
bringing a cavalcade of blind and bunged-up companions,
all denied redemption, feeling somehow second class because
they managed to survive, something they would never reveal to outsiders,
conscious that bravery and heroism was now benchmarked as death—
'he paid the ultimate sacrifice' did not apply to those un-enshrined—
as monument committees wept under eucalypts
on furious summer mornings that promised only drought and fire.

The night fades late to crooked skies busted as a three pound note.
Down streets cold as charity, echoes of stilettos on parquet floors counterpoint
shanked half-bottles drummed, staccato, against bricks.
Post-war boredom and the emptiness of reconstruction
weighed heavy as a bale of damp wool.
For a time, he sought solace in paid company,
then the listless skin-spin, the shrinking into indifferent doorways
for momentary relief became too much, becoming revolted by who he was.
Escaping himself, he somehow found his own path
out of the prison of rehabilitation—
war service home and job guaranteed for life, he moved west, no regrets—
no family left to mourn, his older brother dead at El Alamein,
mother dead from grief, father dead from the bottle,
leaving behind the meagre hospital rations, the calloused pallets,
the stench of severed limbs and the groans of dying men,
ignoring the pleas of those who begged for death;
keeping only his father's ancient silver timepiece and
the little he could carry in his battered leather port—
unknown at last, damaged just enough to be accepted
riding the streets of his Grainstrip hometown,
carrying its secrets in the mail bags strapped to his bicycle
for twenty-five years, fodder for boys with gings,
drunks and marauding town dogs—riding out to the reserve

on kid money day, seeing the smiles of the children—
on those days he might take out a bag of lollies,
not comprehending the townsfolk's fear of those bright faces,
though he understood their fear of other things—
the dust in vacant shop fronts growing heavier by the hour;
farmers rain-baking under softened brims in frizzling rain,
always insufficient or too plentiful—
the Grainstrip dying inside out, fruit of the poisoned citrus,
closure of the detention centre the final nail in the coffin
of the latest Bright Future, sheep's back broken and weevils in the wheat.

His eyes close once more to inhabit bittersweet memories, breaking down
the litany of depression and dispossession—examining another life,
his own—recalling the sudden pleasure of desire,
the taste of lust in a wanton mouth,
the funky subtle rut of orgiastic pleasure,
her fingertips twined and gently riffling the curls on his upper arm;
how he imagined he loved that girl—yet, in truth, knowing nothing of love—
a courtship spun from the twin strands of self-deception,
her pregnant desperation and his physical need,
mitigated on his part by analysis of his scarred prospects,
culminating in hymns and vows that rang true as pyrite and lasted
as long as the deck of playing cards dancing down main street
when the south-westerlies scream across the plains
scattering sheep and children to shelter.
Winter was bitter, empty streets cold as a meat freezer,
bronchitis nagging unmercifully at his lungs each morning.
Then Molly's child, their child, was stillborn,
a wreath of deformity clutching the poor infant's chest—
maimed like his father, the talk would go,
inferring guilt by transference;
broken apart by tragedy, spring provided no respite;
speech stultified and conversations resented,
the marital bed abandoned, she took refuge in society,
he took refuge in the hotel, adopting a safe role as

scorer for the darts team, staying carefully in the background
though having a reason to be there—in the end, they are
separated in all but name.

He has a one-schooner table, settled in a corner, back to the pub wall,
where he reads the daily paper with the solitary drink he consumes
for others long gone—it is no homage to her memory, Molly's memory,
for that was twenty years earlier, his illusions long disintegrated
by time that may have measured milliseconds,
eternal milliseconds that felt as slow as winter on his scarred face,
just a sage nod to the background symphony
of beer and bullshit in the main bar.
Not long before, they had watched the moon landing here,
gathered before opening time, a great leveller,
as squatter and shearer together observed the fantastical event,
equally mesmerised and elevated in spirit; he is welcomed here,
acknowledged as pariah, a keeper of unmentioned secrets,
purveyor of secret news, assignations, rendezvous—
skewed to rude awakenings, he knows the little tricks
that lovers play all too well—the familiarity of deceit
that picks at restless painful scabs with lusty fingernails
delivering delicious pleasure pangs;
the respectable country ladies, hair-sprayed shut and sharply starched
politely mourned his disfigurement in every sideways glance,
unable to contain their opinions, reinforcing his desire for artifice,
creating his solitary persona, the discarded man—
the fallible, dispossessed man—
who will not know again the touch of a woman;
fidgeting in church, between tea and immortality,
he envisions the execution of falsehoods and dalliances,
issued through adulterated correspondence, sympathy cards;
invitations intercepted, withheld and re-issued to unlikely recipients or
rejected with volatile and impolitic language,
cheques no longer in the mail, returned to addresses
in foreign climes, anonymous allegations sent to newspapers,

pornography sent to church members, rumours of
impending foreclosures, fashioning a new set of truths through his direct actions
drawing a curtain of pain around the town—
causing parlour unrest, unfettered hysteria, insidious mysteries,
tear-soaked bridal veils and doubts corrupting fevered minds;
undetected, yet in open view, revenge is sharpened—
he conceives and devises a whimsical punishing god
more disruptive than any communist agitator, patient and dangerous,
fracturing the social fabric,
their dismissiveness of him matched by his own contempt for them,
challenging their haughty superiority, knowing their private lamentations;
rumours of curses persisting; premonitions of doom
become self-fulfilling prophecies, the strange foreboding that
bad news is coming, creating inconsolable discontent—
he is mesmerised by the ease of his deception.
Vicarious pain drives the priest to drink.

The bicycle clips clatter for an instant on the sideboard,
the final act of a day's work completed; the newspaper rests temporarily nearby,
holding word of a postal strike. Later, he will cast a desultory eye over its pages.
Musty ephemera clings to him, mouldy like religion.
The house has the flattened, fletched look of an isolate's dwelling,
cleansed in pine antiseptic by paid cleaners who adhere to its spartan regime;
blue uniform with its red trim carefully stowed, he sits on his back verandah.
Scudding rain lurches across the plains in a freezing swell of sodden air;
he winces at the thought of the cold on his hip.
Opening the rounded tin, he lifts it slowly to his nose,
inhaling the fragrant scent of fresh tobacco,
luxuriating in the pungent, earthy feel as he
folds it into his palm rolling the tobacco into wafer thin paper;
he flicks the lighter once, smoking his cigarette,
enjoying the swell of smoke easing the tension in his chest,
just as he has always done, taking himself back to Ploughman's Rise,
for it was there that his Molly and the Johnson boy crashed,
eloping in the Johnson family car, missing the bend and

hitting the old flowering gum, car wrecked and petrol leaking;
a wafer-thin missive and an empty wardrobe all that
she had left behind, no trace at all of her essence remained.
The Johnson boy's vacant eyes had spoken his fate,
while Molly had lain trapped, still alive, her plaintive plea for help
falling on ears no longer capable of hearing,
on a heart no longer capable of listening
to anything except the sound of his revenge upon the world,
for then he flicked the match that ignited
the car like a bonfire, impervious to her desperate cries or
to the single hand outstretched in supplication;
so this, his last cigarette of the day becoming his unapologetic ritual-
closing his eyes, he is free-wheeling, machine-oiled,
unchained, down Wattle Creek Hill back into civilisation,
away from memories of eucalypt and petrol burning his nostrils
with its flaring stain, the taint of damaged flesh, the spurned attention—
she constructing the fuse, he lighting the flame—ending all pain.
Some evenings, he flirts with confession, the vision
of seeing his confessor's face alight with shocked understanding
creating a fleeting sense of euphoria, but he resists this impulse;
perhaps his journal will be his confession instead;
eventually, breathing deeply and calmly,
with a last considered glance across the paddocks,
he extinguishes his cigarette.

# Jumpers
Bronwyn Rodden

There've been five jumpers since I started here, bit of a hazard working near The Gap. Last Friday night our new girl came across one on her way out for the weekend; very upset. We don't try to talk to them, call the police and ambulance. What if we said the wrong thing…

It's so beautiful, the Gap, you can see why. The only non-jumper I've seen was a young woman full of sleeping pills and gin, curled up in a bunker burnt red by the sun in all the hours she was there. It's usually tourists that find them.

L, pretty, smart, funny, found her boyfriend, who had a habit of slapping her around giving her a bit of biff, clocking her, rearranging her face, knocking her senseless, doing her grievous bodily harm, was playing around. She got dumped when she complained about his affair on the side, then tried to top herself.

She's at her Dad's now. Where do people go when their parents die?

Alcoholism's like a slow suicide, it's all giving up. You give up easier if there's a promise of something better beyond. Some start heading for that better life as soon as they hit the wall of adulthood, leaving the rest of us with this one.

I guess the beauty of the theory is that if there isn't anything, they'll never know.

Success, money, parenthood, career, it's all up to you, and the measure of success has an inflation rate that would even scare an economist.

Come for dinner? Thai, Indian, Mexican, Vietnamese, Japanese, African, Burmese, Creole Cajun, Vegetarian, Macrobiotic, Vegan, Modern Australian…

Have you got all the ingredients? Are they: fresh, organic, fat-free, sugar-free, high in anti-oxidants, low in cholesterol and gluten, free of hormones, non-genetically altered, grown in sympathy with the environment, native to Australia, purchased from a sound outlet, not packed in unrecyclable bags… Would you like tea or coffee? Darjeeling, Orange Pekoe, Irish Breakfast, English Breakfast, Green…

You noticed something about J—pretty, dark-haired, lively, straight off— it was her voice, too loud and edgy, then she'd seem to realise and the words would fade away. It took hours to tell her it was ok when she'd made a small mistake, and that it was fine. But she made no sense of 'fine', any mistake was as big as Centrepoint Tower to her and nothing you said mattered. It was her head-space and you could never see it from inside.

Self-actualization is only good if the self creates enough excitement once its actualized. What if it's just ordinary? J moved to another floor about a year ago, then changed jobs. She suicided last week, funeral's tomorrow. She leaves a young son and a husband, confused. Babies, those beautiful perfect toys are popping out of young bellies into a world some parents loathe, all over the place. Unfortunately, they grow into adults, not just bigger babies, mostly.

V tells us he's seen bone-pointing at work—it's scary. There's one thing to remember, if the pointer is less powerful than the pointee it could be a disaster and the pointer ends up dead. D pointed the bone, she told me, and sure enough, the woman died. Suicide, just before the cancer got her. But things started happening much earlier, maybe before D, maybe there was another bone. D has a lot of energy, she was angry, she could make things happen.

A man from the office walked down town one lunchtime and didn't come back. We all started walking down town, wondering if he'd pop up from behind a clump of trees, or had gone to Brisbane. There's a gradual migration of people which begins, they say, in Western Australia and works its way around the coast, ending in Queensland. One day there'll be so many on the move, they'll create a weather effect, like El Nino, and blow us all up to Cairns.

He'd been uneasy too, had an edginess hanging about him like flu.
We all wondered: a woman, we'd think, abduction, rape, murder.
A man? Broad daylight? It was a fine day, clear blue sky and warm;
a good day to disappear. Week after week, nothing. The nothing
was hard to take in. A person breathes, talks, walks, and has to eat.
But his accounts weren't used, he was ceasing to exist through finance.
We'd look at the fences and shops he would have seen
As he walked down town, and wondered.

They found him months later, after the fires cleared the bush.
Couldn't tell how he died. Someone said they'd seen him
a week after he disappeared, then a few days later near some shops.
They estimated he may have walked around thinking about it for two weeks.

In 1851 Sarah (8) Jane (6) Emily (3) and Joseph (18 months) all died within a month.
They are now thin lines on a single tombstone, one death a week for four weeks,
four trips to the cemetery to open the grave. There's little left of lives so short.
Their mother died 16 years later. 16 years without her little children
all rotting in the ground before her. Father, a further 8 years on.
Joining their beloved children in Paradise, or something like that.
It's a fair bet and we all hope it came true for them, they had little luck
this side of the grave… No wonder Catholics like to gamble.

The taxi driver yesterday had only been on the job for six months;
he still found it interesting enough to talk about. At the casino, men
went mad and broke jaws in anger as they waited for a car.
A young mother told him she was looking for her husband who hadn't
been home in two days. High rollers could do it, he said, and win,
but you had to have the money to lose. If you had enough, you could
keep betting till you won. The odds always come around eventually
If you could wait till 'eventually'…

71

One man, sick of everything sold his house, business, took his $500,000 down to the casino to make one bet. Win or lose that was all he'd do. Roulette, he bet on the colour—50:50 chance, double your money: he won—he left. He was one in a million.

The taxi driver picked up a prostitute at the Cross this morning, $50 she said, was all she'd made. Standing on William Street all night in the cold for $50.
He picked up another woman, respectable, but slurring, not drunk, he thought, probably drugs. She was crying, wanted to go to Watson's Bay. He was wary.
No not The Gap, she did live there. But on the way, she started taking off her clothes, one piece at a time, and tossing them out the window. He was worried but she seemed otherwise OK. Pantihose, shoes, all went out the window. When they got to her house— very nice too—she had no money. He didn't make a fuss, was worried how it would look.

They're changing the colour of the Casino buses from black to white, black being unlucky for Chinese people. And all the number plates have an 8 in them— a lucky number for the Chinese—and there's a door to door pick up service: Cabramatta to Casino. A man who'd lost $400,000 went nuts on the taxi queue, was held down, then collapsed. He was OK. The security officers gave the driver a cab charge to take him home to Marrickville. He didn't want a doctor.
My driver met a guy who only bets by numbers on the horses—trifectas, does ok. I tried with the number of the taxi. The first few weeks, nothing, Then it happened, a trifecta paid $1200 for $2. Then…

72

The Diceman of the Seventies was superseded by the toss of the coin of the Eighties.
When everything gets too complicated, keep it simple, said the Behaviorists.
To make your decision, spin your coin, if you liked what comes down, do it,
If not, you really wanted the other. Decision made.
Complicate—simplify; Process —action; Confusion—clarity; Responsibility —toss of a coin…

There was a movie about people seeking purpose who ended up
seeking death. It will clarify, said the guru, if people don't really
want to go, they will come back. Oh yeah? I asked a psychologist
what he thought about God. He said he took an each way bet.

We were in Ireland way up in the north country, fabulous green
all around us, with my cousin, looking at a shrine: a pile of old church
stones, half a wall and a small box with a cross in it. People had left all sorts
of things there for luck; medals, coins, a tie; we stood, smug smiles
on our faces as my cousin tossed in a coin. 'You never know'.

The thing about J was that no matter how hard you tried
you could never convince her that everything was all right.
If she made the tiniest mistake she'd apologise over and over

and look really worried. She wasn't stupid, she knew someone would come and tell us not to get concerned, and it seemed all right. But inside you knew she'd never forgive herself, no-one could ever forgive her enough for her to believe it. If only we could laugh about it, tell her ok, she held onto things we didn't, but couldn't she find another box to put them in besides the one for serious things? Sometimes you'd start to believe her, that it was more dire than we thought, she was so convincing. She must have amassed so much unforgiveness that there was no room left in the box for anything else.

I don't remember ever seeing her laugh. Laughter, they say, has only been acceptable recently. For centuries it was discouraged, the province of fools and women and other low sectors of society. Now it's used to heal. When it's all too complicated and silly, laugh. If only it could be turned on like a tap. Or as easy as tossing a coin….

# To Ilumine
## the imagined book, a Qur'an 1555 AD/CE

Robyn Rowland

> *Beautiful writing makes the truth clearer.*
> Alī ibn Abī Ṭālib
> cousin and son-in-law of Muhammad (c 596-661)
> *Calligraphy is the tongue of the hand.*
> ʿAbd Allāh ibn al-ʿAbbās
> Companion of the Prophet (c 619-688)


I


Simply to begin here—the desire to worship.
Offer gifts of beauty, begin plain, but
embroider, embellish, swoop and colour,
perfect a craft to glitter down centuries.
The aim of this art is to praise.

The reed pen is in Ahmed Karahisari's hand,
calligrapher's eye sharp as the nib that when worn
must be cut back to the exact size or all is flawed.
Beside him, a writing tray of carved walnut,
inlaid with ivory and mother-of-pearl.

Small knives lay ready for the trimming task,
his ivory *makta* to hold them, each chip reverently
caught in a small bowl. Ceramic ink-pots are brimful
with lampblack ink that never fades and others of
burnt beeswax, pine and linseed oils, gum and soot,

their dark depths aching for the light of the page.

Ivory spalls, carved paper cases of golden inlay,
paper sheers to slice the paper, await. He waits.
For the way, for the tongue to speak, shadow of
the hand behind the hand. Divine thought held
by words can only be attempted, never known.

He understands that space left is as significant
as space used. Yet the glory of the words call to him
for embellishment. Pages of script pile on his desk
as they dry; verses of the holy book black with clarity
emerging from his spiritual geometry, inner meaning

to the inner meaning of the text humming inside his inks.
Outside these palace workshops the gardens are
buzzing with banter, harem quiet behind grilles,
and the afternoon opens to him as the blank pages
that have lain one year in the dark, readying.

Yet not blank. Merely untouched by him.

II

By him. But not by his young companion of the book,
Şebek Memet Efendi, already Master of Ebru,
paper marbling, preparing sheet on sheet as he does today.
Horsehair brushes tied to rose stems, needles and combs
lie ready, all tools to part and shape the paints on the
face of the water, dyes mixed and viscous with ox-bile.

Pomegranate, walnut skins, seeds of buckthorn,
leaves of indigo, and earth itself, all crushed and
powdered on marble, flank the tray of unknotted
pine wood. Soft water will be hardened a little with
gum of the tragacanth, orchid-root too expensive this season.
In the ebru basin's fluid face he watches for stillness.

Within and without, the hand that holds the paint to be
sprinkled, needs to know peace, reverence for the act,
love for the art. He thinks: this page is for the Holy One,
'the book being read repeatedly'. No work of beauty
will emerge unless he enters the tranquillity of a dervish.
Though young, he knows that. Patience is entrance.

Loosing colours, drop by drop, he separates, swirling
them with care, seeing again the Divine. Paper is laid
into the tray, rested wet, slid out with his breath.
Exquisite cream, tea-dyed so as not to tire his friend's
eyes during his calligraphy, the sand-marbled heart
of the sheet glows, while the extremity of each page

in porphyry marbling is veined rose pink.
Glazed with a moon's sigh of egg white, later
he will polish it with agate, its sheen, flint-bright.
End-papers will arise mauve from crushed purple
logwood; tulips purse their lips out of the skins of onions.
On the top corners of each page, passionflower designs

will unfurl in caramel from dark brown soot
gathered out of the chimneys of confectioners.
He understands too many hues might
risk confusion but he knows the flow of layers
in colour deepen vibrancy, brighten the heart.
Page One and its end page for the new Qur'an.

III

It is to those end sheets the calligrapher turns now.
A large leaf of the poplar, treated and resting one year,
has been fixed there, carries the soul of the tree to the world,
mimics the shape of the human heart. His mind glides along
Arabic letters for a form his service might take—

    the swoop of a bird in flight—
    stark leg of a stork balancing—
    ocean's ancient curl that once
    Phoenicians swept into shape—
    light nib curving right to left,

angled to press wide or slight according to careful pressure—
    he begins.

IV

Today the *müzehhip*, illuminator, arrives with his gold-leaf,
beaten and mixed into a perfect blend of water and gum
            —not too thin, not gelatinous—
His mind is bursting with flowers from Topkapi Palace,
spring gardens blooming with thousands of
jonquils, narcissi, irises, hyacinths, roses, tulips—
he will press into life in the first fine pages.

He thinks the margins beyond the *cedvel*, borderlines
of the page, might take thin spirals of Indian indigo
and powdered lapis. The final page might open upon
clouds fringed with silver over roses pink as sunset.
He understands too much gold might seem excessive
yet how else to create awe for the gift of holy words,
embellish, so time will not dust them away?

V

The book binders are ready.
Upper and lower inside covers will be card
covered in watered-silk with gold and silver thread,
storks flying over cherry and orange blossom.
Coloured silks are threaded to sew everything into unity.
Leather already seasoned, *nevregen* sharpened
to add their *kaa't** to the book,
binders carve a relief of tulips barely open
into the leather outer cover burnished copper,
leaves twining across the spine in fine filigree.
Wrapped finally in velvet, its scent rises—
something of leaf, of forest and earth.

VI

An apprentice to Sinan, the great palace architect, has designed a box
to house this book, so magnificent it stands the height of a man's waist.
Dazzling, its orchestration of inlay and inner tortoise-shell is polished
to a carmine glow. Hexagonal, its walls are geometric slices of ebony
with tongue and groove of shell and walnut wood, a contrast of dark and
light, mahogany and ivory. Its domed lid shines red with cinnabar insets,
a shattering of starbursts in inlaid mother of pearl, iridescent as the soul.

He knows a plain box of walnut would hold the book, yet
his worship of materials smooth in his palms demands
inclusion if wonder is to be continuous from page to cupboard.

And for a Sultan such as Suleiman Kanuni,
who builds a library of eleven thousand books,
whose own *ghazals* as Muhibi, the lover,
shame the word 'flourish', pouring their praises
richer than *nar* syrup, spilling across the page
their love for God, for his beloved Hürrem Sultan—
He, who decorates the land with mosques of awe,
He, who holds the Holy Book his closest guide—
no artisan from the *Ehl-i Hiref*, 'Community
of the Talented', could do less with his craft.

Or else, why an artisan be?

*Kaa't art; *nevregen* small, sharp knife used to carve into paper, leather; *Nar*, pomegranate

79

**Notes:**

**Ahmed Karahisari,** 15-16th century master Ottoman calligrapher 1468–1566.

**Şebek Memet Efendi.** Ebru Master about which little in known. Work mentioned in oldest book written about ebru is a treatise entitled 'Tertib-i Risale-i Ebri', dated 1608. Seems to have worked on Fuzûlî, poetry *Hadîkat üs-Süedâ (Garden of pleasures)* in 1595.

**Mimar Sinan : Koca Mi'mâr Sinân Âğâ** (c. 1489/1490 – July 17, 1588) chief Ottoman architect and civil engineer for sultans Suleiman the Magnificent, Selim II, and Murad III.

This Sultan was known as Suleiman The Magnificent to the West (1494-1566); Suleiman Kanuni (The Lawgiver) to his Ottoman Empire. Under his patronage, hundreds of imperial artistic societies (*Ehl-i Hiref,* 'Community of the Talented') were administered in Topkapı Palace. After an apprenticeship, artists and craftsmen could advance in rank within their field and were paid commensurate wages in quarterly annual installments. Earliest documents from 1526 list 40 societies with over 600 members. The *Ehl-i Hiref* attracted the empire's most talented artisans to the Sultan's court, both from the Islamic world and conquered territories in Europe, resulting in a blend of Islamic, Turkish and European cultures. Artisans in service of the court included painters, poets, musicians, book binders, furriers, jewellers and goldsmiths.

# Displaced

## Vuong Pham

i.

Thrust to a distant continent
and the clouds keep creating
the shape of our motherland
Vietnam
at the refugee camp
with nothing but the dirty clothes on our backs
taste of urine in our mouths
there was no other choice, it was the ale
we produced for ourselves to sustain our lives
crossing the South China Sea
where fates were uncertain and erratic as the ocean
waves swirling around like death
though this body of water was a portal
that needed venturing, in the hope of discovering peace

ii.

Upon arrival the Sisters of Mercy
gave us oranges, cut into the shape of boats
that sweet taste of freedom
from fruit that grew in a distant field
where the sun shone beyond our perception
in the autumn
susurration of palm leaves
from the living room window of our first house
decrepit, patches of sunlight seeped through
shattered bits of glass
depicting fragments of memory
of at least having each other
I thought my cousins were my brothers and sisters
crowded under one roof

crowded like cargo on the refugee boat
I was young and oblivious to the war
my childhood, peaceful like our front yard
a clean slate
guarded by the palm trees that stood like regal priests
there must have been a higher palm
that protected this side of the earth
like my mother
tucking her children in and telling bedtime stories
in the gentle breeze
father sometimes drank sitting on the veranda
at twilight, at the going down of the sun
looking back in the direction of Vietnam
his head among the space
between stars
thinking of his family eating rice dinner
worried about knocks on their door
and disappearing into the night
thinking of the ghosts of his conscripted friends
lost in the jungle
yet our parents would console each other
knowing their children would live a better life
from the veranda's view, a golden river
parts two ways

iii.

Mother stitched together the torn threads
of my childhood
blue teddy bear
put its smile back
created home-made clothes patched
from the cheapest range of fabric
a Singer
that reverberated like a machine gun through late nights
fighting hard from empty pockets
fighting hard for our future

sometimes at night I'd look out the window
thinking the stars are repair holes
waiting to be threaded into infinite possibilities
through the tapestry of our dreams
though I remember going to a family portrait shot at school
we wore clothes my mother sewed
pupils asked us if we were wearing pyjamas
our lives unassimilated
classified like a pinned bug in a display case

iv.

At school lunchtime
when I brought *bún thịt nướng*
with smelly fish sauce
they ran away from me
*banana, chink eye, gook, bring that back to Vietnam*
I forced myself to eat Vegemite
my tongue's pain disguised
by fake smiles
so I could fit in
but I was always left out
of the playground gossip
among the scurrying of leaves in the wind
my dreams of belonging lost in the grass
I think of my countrymen
of all the bodies
face down in the dirt
of all the houses torn down to their skeletons
spiritless in their company

v.

My brother and I fought once
over a breadstick with cheese dip
dad got so angry
he kicked the snack box like it was the head of his enemy

dumped it in the bin
he had to escape the war in his country
didn't have time for our petty little battle
the silence of fallen soldiers echoed through the empty hallway

vi.

Days later, my brother was sick
I skipped catching the bus home that day
to avoid bullies
I should've just given him the cheese cracker
to ward off the virus
father picked me up later
on the way home he raised his fist in the air
telling me to be strong
and stand up to bullies
though he could not stand against
the Communist oppressors of his hometown
kicking down the doors of people's freedom
he was right
what if noodles tasted better than bread?
what if I didn't have to keep trying to widen my eyes?
what if my skin colour was not a banana, but yellow
like the colours of the true Vietnamese flag?
yellow like the rising sun

vii.

I woke up, it was Vietnam
the once great nation
in my dream
Vietnam before 1975
that yellow flag flowed in the free breeze
at the Saigon market
among the *hoa mai vàng* trees in full bloom
covered in the light of *Tết*
my mother wears a traditional *áo dài*

singing a bygone song
about a yellow-chested bird
perched atop a bamboo grove
happily chirping
*I love my country, I love the people, I love to study*
among Southerners joining in
a melody of kindness
that will surpass all the powers of war
sung in my native tongue
though with words I don't fully comprehend
yet feel the depths of its sentiment
in an ancient glade
accumulating light

viii.

The night before father departs
the country he has spent his whole life
he sits in the church
where he was training to become a priest
vandalised from soldiers
stamping out another perspective
bullet holes of moonlight
shine through the stained-glass depiction of Moses
faced with death in all directions
leading his people to safety
through the exodus
he prays on his knees for all the millions without a shepherd
to set them free
for children were forced to sing songs of a false god
of pharaoh, of *Bác Hồ*
in a land where the red moon never set
upon the waters
of the baptismal font
reflecting this upside-down world
he prays for Vietnam's soul
sent back to the dark ages

praying for a chink of light
upon a homeland
where souls are filled
as wine in a chalice

ix.

Give back to Australia
our parents would say
caressing the side of our cheeks
under a sky collecting stars
where we'd pray each night
thinking of our ancestors
cupping our hopes and dreams
in the promised land of plenty
where the moon's boat shines earnestly
sailing through the ocean of the night sky

x.

Eternity waits
through the countless doors and corridors of time
of each generation
paradise is now
the sun will always shine
above the temporary illusion of any cloud
a psalmist will sing songs
that will echo through the caves of genealogy
our spirit a *Chim Lạc* that can fly away
touch the source of the godly
our hearts are the true asylum
etched with scriptures of truth
that we are unique, not a repeat
a constant reminder
that we are specially handcrafted
by a hand in the sky beyond our perception
fearfully and wonderfully made

# After

## Kevin Smith

*' ... we are well advised to keep on nodding terms with the people we used to be, whether we find them attractive company or not.'*
—Joan Didion

After the break-up, we ended up in Queanbeyan, my two-year-old son and I. Snow-bearing clouds hung above a grey city. We moved into a share house with Wendy. Where we slept, a tin room out the back, tacked on like an after-thought. Cold air rose through holes in the floorboards, and condensation trickled down the iron walls. We slept beneath crocheted blankets Wendy lent us, the morning air smoky with our breath.

2  I rose before the sun to drive my boy to a daycare mum, and myself to work in a timber yard where the mercury only rose above zero after midday, when the fog had lifted. I wore long-johns under my jeans. Timber iced with frost chilled my fingers.

3  Sometimes Wendy looked after him.

4  Once, she came into my room; her nakedness gleamed in pre-dawn light, in frigid air; I took the warmth her body offered—such softness there—not knowing yet how broken I'd become, how incapable of love. And I too dumb, too stunned, to comprehend what I was doing.

5  I'd bought a booster seat from Vinnies, and a seven-hundred-dollar ute with a broken heater, and a rusty floor you could see the road through. I packed our things and left. We drove non-stop to Bathurst. I was going back to university, you see.

**6** I rented in a district outside town. Beyond its scant streets, empty paddocks and desolate hills. Dust drifted through the cottage's hollow rooms, its windows thick with grime; it had the smell of neglect about it.

**7** My friend Pam, she lived up the road.

**8** I waited for the semester to begin, and walked the bush. He led the way, my son, and picked up sticks too big for him. A pair of wedge-tailed eagles dropped from a winter sky to strip a dead wether's bones of meat.

**9** We stood on a bridge, the two of us, above a railway line laid down these thousands of miles to the other side of the continent. I imagined her on that train, a blurred face in a window. His chubby fingers gripped the mesh fence, and he leaned into my leg. A hot wind rushed up between the boards, the stench of diesel, the exhaust chugging black rags into the air. He watched the train disappear around a sweeping bend, and looked at me, the wheels on the iron rails keening a lament.

**10** When the rain came, we gathered mushrooms in a bucket he dragged through wet paddocks.

**11** He didn't ask about his mother. At night, I read him stories.

**12** When the sun rose he woke me, his small hands trailing over my eye-lids. He led me to the bathroom. We'd shopped in town the day before. In dirty bath water, oranges floated like moons. On the bottom, a sodden loaf of fruit bread.

**13** We walked to the post office. The shop was shut.

**14** One day, Wendy drove the dirt street pluming dust. I stood on the porch, and leaned against a timber post. I heard her close the car's door, and I nudged a piece of busted concrete off the porch.

**15** We stood in the yard, the weeds pushing up the pavers, the woodshed door banging in a breeze.

**16** I wandered into the afternoon to search for the words to say to her. I walked about the house. And she was somewhere else.

**17** The clouds thinned. The sun lowered in the western sky. All there was, was the wind.

**18** Wendy left.

**19** My friend Pam came down. We stood on the porch and watched the dust settle, and the sun glimmering on the horizon. She was lovely, is what Pam said. I said nothing. Somewhere in the house, my son sat on a lino floor with a shoebox full of trucks and cars; engine noises wafted out an open window.

**20** He came out, gave me a car, and went back in.

**21** A crow stepped a barbed-wire fence, then flew off, its cry dying on the evening air. Pam looked at me. Looked up the road. Then went home.

**22** The silence left behind, unbearable.

# The Quiet Patience of The Street

Robyn Rowland

Sun hits the deck tiles over sea views
that never change, never stay the same.
And at six o'clock we gather each to
our own kitchen, steamers and easy soups,
in the street where I was raised.
Dinners are early here now.

Next door, Marg is weary, her husband worn by
fierce nightmares, Parkinson's, diabetes and more.
Conscripted at eighteen, shipped to war in
Vietnam, 1960's, he was sprayed with defoliant
Agent Orange by our American allies, as
we were dragged *all the way with LBJ.*

Across the road, Paul carries his love
up the front stairs, her ovarian cancer
well-bloomed, making her lighter than
the prayers he leads in church on Sunday.
His four daughters blossom, anxious.
It is Christmas and the tree still untrimmed.

Down the road, Pat lives alone now, still young.
His wife squeezed by that same seed cancer,
passed away last winter, all her musical gift intact.
Sometimes he goes out with a boat, in a car,
in hope for some kind of respite. *A hard year,
the last one,* he tells me. *Random life,* we agree.

Back home, caring, I watch my father in his
new old-age, just now at one hundred years.
Impossible to grasp that. Glad for it.
His lovely heart is wearing, but not his humour.
*I don't know why I'm so tired.*
*And I don't want you to tell me!*

We sing robustly with Richard Tauber from the 40s,
*Goodbye* from the *White Horse Inn.* He remembers it
clearly, and all the old Patterson poems
he grew me up on. But not the date or those who called
this morning. Kindly, I repeat answers over and over
every day, because, we belong here, in this patient street.

# Newcastle Impermanent

## Greg McLaren

'Driving over Styx Creek, appropriately' *

'Nothing ever happens to people like us/ Except we miss the bus' ^

Non-locals always say how beautiful
it is, meaning the vineyards—the *wineries*,
we called them—having them so close
to hand, like a convenient cocktail waiter
stashing away his or her tips
to buy some painting time, and who,
you later find out through a surprise
back-channel, is working to revivify
photorealism as part of a fine-grained,
ironising, but not actually ironical stance,
but you also know these visitors haven't ventured yet
out to where poverty's tenacious as a colony,
where something else always is or isn't
happening, and sure isn't happening to them.

\*\*\*

Under that monotonous-seeming past's a slack pile of broken
tiles slaked with snake skin scrapes and dirt, once
in dire need of a regrout: a fever dream of
cracked voices, those long, deep vowels and extinguished

terminal consonants of footy or dog tracks slipping
into castrato a sec; and in there there's a long
hard fearful rank of work boots and bureaux leaning on,
squeezing down final dark breathy larynxes, bloating and making

silent the tongues district-wide. Underneath, even deeper,
a slow shaking, subsonic but measurable:
loosens the district's deepest piers, it moves around and flexes

the sunspots and lesions its skin's upside has always shown.
Something's fallen down, another translucent else is sudden
in its place, all depending on exchanges recorded but unseen.

***

Think about it, go on.
The Mullet Festival's not that far
from TINA, not really, especially not if
your driving DNA's locally sourced.

The tute room's windowless
and in it sit students from South
Dakota, some random hills suburb
of Adelaide, and South Sudan,

Merewether, Avalon. Blokes ute it in
from Lorn, Morpeth and Pelaw Main
to chew strategy at Sticky Rice, at Moor,

discard the sushi option, as *it's too
fucken bogan*, as the one in the Angels
t-shirt fairly quietly comes out to his da.

***

At the house on Dent Street, at the first birthday party
for the twins of Pete's something to do with his work,
there're several well-designed but very casually supervised
games for the older kids near the unfenced pool
and a pretty much civil conversation about the almost
local appeal—note the slight displacement?—
of One Nation: *A lot of people up there are genuinely disaffected,*
says the car panel entrepreneur: *they feel left out of all the money
coming in to the district. And the conversation*: deep calm voice.
*Well, maybe that's why they tell me to shut up and piss off home*
(the Scone-born registrar with Pakistani grandparents
on her mum's side). And I butt in with, *Look, I went to school
with Brian Burston's son—honestly, fuck Cessnock,
it's another town with lots of people but not enough surnames.* Or wish I had.

***

These people, I don't know where
they come from, they keep putting things up,
pulling and knocking them down, burning them
like they were trying to manage Country,
I don't know, *razing*, they call it, trashing
their own shit with fire and starting again, one thing
on top of the other, one style on top of the other,
not looking like none of it's planned at all, building too
on top of where the water comes from,
feeding the old springs to their animals
and then they're gone—spring and animal—
and you know, they get mawkish about that, as if
it somehow happened *to* them, they stay put in the one place,
have no manners for Country, and they won't learn the language.

\*\*\*

I'll sing to you of Bolwarra, Telarah,
Tenambit, of Louth, Lorn and Morpeth,
the sweep of the river and of the highway;
of the curling railway through St Martins Creek,

High Street, Victoria Street, East Maitland,
the ferrying the train does of junkie parents,
their sons with the faces of boxers,
the daughters so furious and still

in their unicorn tops sizes too big,
and but for the grace of, go I.
The silvery needling track sings out
of Warabrook, of Waratah in the wheedling

idiom of smack, after that warm golden feel,
snug in the curve up ahead you don't see.

\*\*\*

I don't really want to say tentacles
because of the obviousness, but
I will. I have to. It's what I mean. The cathedral's outlasted
the steelworks (spumes of smoke and gas
scope out on the shifts in wind and fade

even as they seep into lungs) and
likely will the mines, the big church's reach
deeper and further than the pits
but not in a way you could measure
unless your metric includes covert talk, buggered

kids, pick your drugs, too much drink,
work, families who don't, and who don't talk because of
those creeping groping tentacles under beds,
under the country, fucking us up, fucking us over.

∗∗∗

*The killer, Lieutenant James Wallis, 1816*

We marched into April     Fires burned
always     A child cries out     Our lines
are rank     In the rocky creek, dogs set up
a howling     Running off in the gun smoke
of flintlocks means over the cliffs
Some children     some women shot
Bodies bounding over the rocks
over the precipice     I was partly
successful     leading two women
three children     away from their dead
Not a blessing     melancholy     Almost
impossible to bury them     I wrote
to the Governor     There would be instructions
In their camp     plundered potatoes     corn

∗∗∗

wheeze for a drink of water     they
give you a drip     in your sick bed
your skin     its natural oils
discolour the sheets

you piss noisily into a cup
the flask I'm holding
trying to read     you revise
your expectations to illustrated westerns

the cover's buxom woman
popping buttons on her cowboy shirt
ping and thwack     ping and thwack

the neighbour's kid throwing the ball against the wall
catching it    thinking he could learn to keep wicket
the month they give you is quite precise

*** 

The little slant-roofed weatherboard
houses, coated with coal dust,
it looks like, and the flag flaps away
its crisp and harrowing shadow
across this one's roof, the windows
either side of the snub door.

He's in his splayed blue dressing gown
and brown slippers, hose in hand,
the careful stone garden, those bare
succulents needing not that much,
echoing, just about, the gasworks'
bulbosity. His fag end twitches,

and a grace accompanies its flight
in a cooling arc to the concrete steps.

*** 

From The Hill they really do
look down on everyone else.
In heavy fog small islands
survive—Merewether Heights

and maybe, far off, the Heights:
Cardiff, Lambton. The names
give it away, self-conscious, as if
topography renders privilege

permanent. Places named after the wrong
people are a problem here, too: Morriset, Wallis
Creek, Lake Macquarie. Don't even mention

Murdering Gully. At Lambton's Skyline
Drive-in, consecutive retro weeks feature
*Rabbit Proof Fence* and *Wolf Creek*.

\*\*\*

I think that's a dog down there on the beach,
weaving together the sea and the swinging shoreline.
Small silver prints stamped there for seconds,
swallowed by a larger silver, foiled by it,
the long swish the ocean's making, has made,
peeling away the sand's skin, slipping it off
and away under the wave-busted light of the sun.

You have to shade your eyes, thought it doesn't
work, or only imperfectly. You looked down only
because something moved at the periphery. When
the moon starts crescenting up over the juts of Redhead,
Dudley, over Glenrock, you'll just go, a scratching
sound over the asphalt, made by thong-stuck grains,
and turning from it, turning your back on it, you'll stay gone.

\*\*\*

With my eye, each page of the street directory,
which is nearly antique, looks like
a spread from a human biology textbook—
this suburb a messy spill of capillaries,

that, a hacked-out, spat-up survey of
bronchioles; or, cross-sectioned, the sub-
dermal colonies BCCs grow. It could be
almost of use, in extreme conditions: when,

say, google maps folds, or when, as they must,
the last servers fail—can I turn then, feeling over
these creases, these folds, the scribbled-on

and-out pages of this obsolete Gregory's,
wearing its apostrophe still when the names
on the street signs here don't.

\*\*\*

Fish and chips, salt, weed, seaweed, coconut oil—
along the five Elizabethan beaches of the district,
their shifting and reflective surface, wrinkled below
the glass frontage of the Merewether clubhouse—sucked in

to that littoral portal of self-regard, we scroll past
our gazing selves in our temporary six packs and botox,
the leathery arrays of lift jobs, a tidal slip and slide
of what was voguish once—clades of mullets

thought extinct, the ghosts of boardshorts past.
The ages and stages exhibited in the sand-
crusted arse cheeks of the polite burning lines

behind the open-air showers and taps,
a rank of slapping cheeks, of both types of thong.
Boxing Day bogans like us, like the river breaching its banks.

* Keri Glastonbury, 'Goodbye to All That'
^ Buzzcocks, *Something's going wrong again*

*The killer, Lieutenant James Wallis, 1816* is a found poem using phrases from Wallis' journal describing
his role in planning and executing the Appin massacre. As a result of his role in this he was subsequently
appointed Commandant of the penal settlement of Newcastle.

# Unfinished

## Susan Garman

*Michelangelo's unfinished sculptures*

We were there to see *David*
everyone was.
He commanded us, this boy
we worshipped at his feet.
I know why
we wanted to be like him.
Triumphant, despite our body
bleeding at the touch of feathers
the sight of leaves.

I turn away, retrace my steps
remembering the green and pink marble
light slicing the rain.
Soon my memory will be white
the colour of notebooks I carried for miles
rocks, raw as the sun
after all this time, they are dust.

The soul, however, is another matter.
It is heaviest when you have nothing in your hands
nothing to show the world, but yourself.
All those photographs as a child
the hours you looked at them
trying to see who you were.
Wool that grew inside of you.
If only I could show you something
other than stories, abandoned,
of people who never lived.

Yet here the unfinished is venerated.
Sometimes, even the broken is beautiful.

The slaves wither in marble
the unfinished stone is reminiscent of fleece,
grey as snow.
People pass them on the way to *David*.
Some pause and look with curiosity
and in truth, discomfort.
The struggle to free the soul from stone
can be hard to witness.
An intimacy some call eternal.
I wonder, if they are simply waking
stretching in the morning
or after a bath.
Undressing, shearing the stubble of the day.

They say Michelangelo saw a figure in a block of marble
and released it.
Creation is in God's hands
we just chip away
as slaves do.

It is a tiring business
being dazzled by art.
People sit on benches
catching their breath.
I too feel faint
from the wounds of stone
the touch of a man
his tutorial on how to carve,
how to become.
It is a type of agony
to spend your life
partially revealed.

On the street, shrubs grow in concrete baths.
I sit on the edge and touch the soil.
The Florentine sun burns me
remembering my body
its grains of sand
the wind slowly blowing them away
from the dunes
left behind
eternally, some may say.

# Autoincorrect
## Craig Smith

I

Let's go, she said, on a date
where we won't contribute
to a large language model of data.
Well, how could I refuse.

She pushed a graphite etched note
across the table and asked
that I wait to unfold it until I am within
the confines of the corrugated iron toolshed
in the back of my garden, she confirmed
via satellite photograph that it is a safe space
in terms of drones being unable to read
through the roofing panels.

We've known each other five months.
She's a computer scientist and I'm not.
We met at a talk on robotic bees
newly built to not so much teach
but rather encourage real bees
to pollinate more efficiently.

II

Her work and the way she lives
is focused on keeping chat bots
in a state of perpetual hallucination.

Here is an example: you ask
the computer what year the
Sydney Harbour Bridge was last rotated

in accordance with industrial protocols
that require the span be turned twice
each decade, and the computer will say
March 2021. It can't admit ignorance
so it hallucinates a logic wrought reality.

III

No surveillance, that's one of
the rules for our date. No cameras
on poles (black plums, skin rubbed
sheer where the eye peers through)
and speaking of fruit no groceries
either, those sensors that track your
gaze across the shelves—not good.

Phones will be left at home and we'll
use cash only and we should wait
until its overcast so clouds blanket our
footfalls. She says we should cross
the road at random intervals, go from
one side of the street to the other
so our behaviours aren't predictable.

IV

If the scraping of our personal data
whilst we are holding hands or similar
is unavoidable, as it so often is, she
encourages obfuscation.

She learned this from a research paper,
you actively volunteer meaningless
strings of junk information en masse so
the receiving software learns nothing.

She said I could just talk as I normally do
and that should be fine, but she might
chat like the wings of a moth, camouflage
her words with layers of banality, like
what happens to the family name Smith if
you try to locate them in a phone book.

V

Ethically I don't know if I should describe
what she is wearing lest a portrait emerges
of her aesthetic references and even brand
names that could build an image catalogue

that profiles her essence.

Perhaps I could describe all that she is not
wearing on our date (pleather, lemonade felt)
so enough negative space remains, a relief
of her presence (withdraw fish bowl earrings)

to see who is left behind.

VI

You might think this level of care
should apply to this poem—why go
to so much trouble to enjoy a date
completely off the record, a meeting
palimpsest scored blank, only to
then map out the architecture of the
whole endeavour.

To which I would respond that, while
I appreciate the compliment, to
think it is within my capacity to truly
know what is happening around
me at any given time, and to accurately
take note of this—it's not the case.

This is really what we don't want computers to learn:
how to not know, how to be eternally uncertain, how
to be full of ontological gaps. That's the secret sauce.

VII

She likes it when I hum copyright free
melodies (I don't tell her they borrow
substantially from Metallica and Bjork,
I'm just waiting for the right moment)

and she hates the idea that a computer would
ever be able to do the same, which they can,
she knows this, she attended a concert of bee
music orchestrated by algorithm, a thousand
mechanical wings fluttering in tuned resonance
(this night changed her, she didn't even mean
to go, she was looking for a Beethoven playlist
and got so far as typing 'Bee' and autocorrect
predicted: well, if you like bees, you'll love this).

VIII

I guide her head beneath a metal crossbeam
hanging between loose wires and an empty
elevator shaft. It is midday in the holoscene.

This carpark was in a state of redevelopment
but then it stopped. A vegetable garden on
Level 6 used to be cared for by an education
centre on the ground floor, but they're gone.

Nobody saw us enter. We are echo's ghosts.

I don't worry so much about chat bots writing
poems like this one, or that they'll improve
the form, because we got here first. Like this
little golden patch of clean light we sit in to
share an orange, and smile, and kiss—

Whatever follows, remember we got here first.

# Report from Sarajevo
Jennifer Kornberger

1.

**We arrive for the conference at the Hotel Europe**
thirty years after the war

shawled women intercept us
beg with soft voices, insistent as the snow.

Upstairs, the Austrian military in combat camouflage
hold talks on security in Eastern Europe

downstairs in the Atrium Hall, six war journalists
sit in front of us to discuss journalism
as the first draft of history

they are not young, not well dressed
they know war and are decorated
for their accounts of it

when they speak
you can see the past rising
in their throats, the present washing
towards it, they are like standing waves
still sifting fact from propaganda

they speak of going to the morgue
lifting the linens to count the bodies themselves
to write *as seen* by Associated Press

of being arrested, detained by their own government
typewriter smashed with a baseball bat
shots fired over the head

the war wolves not wanting to lower morale
by accurate accounts, the editorial policy
the production of hate.

They want to say things about reporting
before the digital age, how Bosnia
was the last war where it was possible
to be a reporter in the way one would wish

they speak now as if to their former
Nikon camera and Olivetti typewriter selves

when they stumped over the slaughter fields
of Srebrenica with their recording equipment

through summer blood, winter blood

when truth still had its alphabet of eyes
when it still had human facial gestures

however grotesque, the texture,
the grain of an old photograph
a pine tree forest smell.

Of course, they wanted to stop the war
with their reporting. They stare
at the university students who are
checking their messages, one moves
his glass of water to the centre
of the low table in front of him

they feared becoming accessories to the war
inspectors of war crimes as they were happening.

There is a mute thickness about their necks
their eyes are clear and dry
but each larynx is weeping

the Atlas bone is weary
their heads teeter like tired planets
some of them have seen nine wars.

The audience is silent, listening to the howl
of the war wolves now rising over the globe.

2.
**In the lunchbreak**
the Austrian soldiers chest themselves
around the streets near the hotel

their camouflage fabric is the latest design—
a blur of tones from grey pink to sap green
hints of violet and yellow
in the form of a pixelated landscape

as if an Impressionist painting
has been fed into a digital
programme, the natural spectrum
become artificially intelligent

the wearer a piece of technology
to be inserted into a scene of conflict

a deadly, out of focus chameleon
not easy to distinguish as human
on any screen.

3.
**In the final session**
a story is offered from the Tribunal
where these journalists testified

where justice was served
year by meticulous Hague year

how, after the thousands of documents,
photographs and footage presented
as incontrovertible evidence of war crimes

the defiant accused rounded on a witness
and demanded, *but aren't you simply lying?*

how the judge brought his hammer down
so hard it broke.

4.
**Someone asks me, so what will you write?**

Several stanzas, stripped of minor hopes
something that has lost the ease of images
a summary, unlyrical, a statement:

every year the war criminals
grow in stature
until they become statues

solid heroes, martyrs who write
the second draft of history

they breed a new species of behaviour—
rival monuments removed by night
the stony refusal to use the word genocide

the judge's hammer lies splintered
over the Balkans

beyond the courtroom
the idea of ethnic cleansing

arises again as if for the first time.

5.
**Of course, I want to stop the war**
with my reporting

to erase the code that is not human
the sequence of prompts that forms the phrase
that attacks truth like a drone.

All I can do is make a practice
of taking a single word, like *neighbour*

a word whose meaning
has been hacked to pieces
and attempt to restore its dignity

make a practice of restlessness
of waking and wandering

of crossing borders
to lift the linens of the world.

6..
**When we leave Sarajevo**
traffic stalls behind a car on the main road
west of the river

the front door hanging open
like an unhinged jaw, no driver

the interior
slowly filling with snow.

# Inside the Image
## Paul Hetherington

'*the opposition between what is seen and what is imagined may be fading*'—Renate Brosch

1.
In this image
old market gardens
are a bright conurbation—

twists of bamboo
slung across swampland
point toward suburbs
still being built,
and crockery's smashed
in a creek's doubtful swill.

An acid-green flower
bleeds viscid sap.
A small, nerve-edged vole
dips a brown snout.

2.
It's rain and roof-rattle
showing a bed
that floats into downpour
yet remains untouched.

3.
The sea slumps across
a patch of sand
like a fat man diving
forwards on his belly.
A girl scoops ice cream
into paper-wrapped cones;

a woman lounges
with her back to a pier.
Light, like seawater,
begins to run
on my sun-exposed arm.

4.
Precise in its detail,
this seems a template
for every old bicycle—
a nicked and scratched frame
black handlebar grips,
a taut, locked chain
and tightly-spoked wheels.
It will never churn dust
in skids and wheelies;
never slide to a halt
at a quarry's edge,
yet the burnished seat
escapes out of paint
as a haze of dark leather.

5.
A house in a cleft
squints across dunes,
a girl on a bike
feels her hair
like dark impasto
or rising dough.
Her father made
a plywood dolls house
before he died,
to carry inside
her beach-housed world.
She remembers surprises
of unwieldy colour,
a serrated wood cake,

chairs in hot pink—
and, also, this painting
hanging askew
on a single nail
when the removalists left,
as if innocence
would never leave with them.

6.
Views of the places
we visited and cherished
have turned to slashes
of a palette knife,
and indelicate strokes
of a split-handled brush—
a lake where a willow
is a penitent praying;
a fox that stands
like a carriage of grace;
and stairs you climbed
while throwing back words
like rivets and nails.
There are also blue sheets
on a flimsy line
like rectangles of summer
after wind-soured days.

7.
This view reveals
outcrops and treelines
above a wide valley,
with a globed, fizzing star
at the edge of the frame.
Penitents gape
at the marvellousness;
birds, now flightless,
fall from air.

But the image shifts
to an out-of-breath traveller
bent over, gasping
and obscured by shadow.
Flakes of paint drop
like snow on the floor.

8.
You walk ahead
in a green overcoat
as a horizon contracts
to intimate blues
through blizzard and snowfall
(at the work's edge
is a wintry platz).
I know you well,
yet how should I see you—
as long brush strokes,
or as someone stepping
away from the paint?

# Library of Leaves
## Jo Gardiner

The museum of lost flight waits inland
from the museum of trees. Beyond

the museum of oceans, along a stream
that once fed maple forests, you find

clear autumn light kept in a strong
container—an edifice of white stone

reinforced against a nuclear winter.
With flickering memories of birds,

and conducted by the flow of clouds,
you arrive at the library of leaves.

Through it, wild geese once flew.
At the end of the building, in a room

faintly lit by the soft, wan glow cast
by deep snow, is the minor museum

of lost flight. All around, felled trees
silently recline. In a glass box,

the small corpse of the last known bird
revolves in the dim. She died

yearning for a mate, though her kind
were long gone. In a strange *fado*,

echoes of her lost song mourn the slow
suffocation of the memory of trees.

◊

My neighbour gave me a Robinia the year you died.

You grew them in a grove where winds divide
two valleys and conjugate the tree's long journey

from the Appalachians to your New England hills.
Named for the Robins—gardeners both—it's prized

for perfumed jam, acacia floral honey, and the way
its bluish leaves turn their cheeks with unspoken

grace. True, if heart rot bores in, tumour-deep,

*

then, hollow at the core, it falls, but its heartwood,
like memory, lives for years beneath the ground,
and survives blue eyes embalmed in the placid light

of May, when, under robinias by the pool, we ate bowls
of berries that stained our lips in that last autumn,

mulled in a blaze of drowning bees. Of all the dialects,
theirs was the thickest tongue sung that day in the rich

drama of your garden. So much to tell you since then,

*

instead, I tell this tree. It stands near my roses, orange

in diamond grooves of bark like lipstick flecks caught
in dried-out skin. You would have hacked the foliage

back by now, refined its yellow elegance down to bone;
I wait. For a last sting of light, for dusk to brush finches

117

into branches before the winds come, when, like a curse
flung from the very root of language, every leaf blown

is another punch thrown to the waiting throat of night.

◊◊

On a morning stamped in gold leaf, the tupelo
   waits at the front gate. Unlike the liquidambar,

she holds—from looping lower boughs—orange
   skirts in half-moon fabric folds that droop

and sweep the ground. It's late in the fall
   after overnight rain has darkened

branches and combed out leaves like sleeves
   dropped from a shoulder, and you can see

the formal structure, how elegant her stature is—
   her ribcage a pagoda of gilded roofs—

*

how she stands aloof, tall, and long boned
   like my grandmother, who, through two wars,

bore her height with a dignity that did not
   stoop with years despite the grief—unknown

to me—she always wore, as a tree would a fire
   burn. A child, I never closed that distance

until one Christmas Eve, with eyes fixed on some
   thing that was not there, she rose and stood

in a cone of lamplight to sing a mourning song
   that dressed with radiance the wound within.

\*

Her wood is pale yellow, the sapwood white.
  Berries in drupes of acidic blue feed the birds,

and greenish flowers, the tiny native bees.
  Now, the low sun swarms in and shakes out

hidden umber: her leaves turn titian and spark
  in scarlet. While the pin oak, the beech and horn-

beam retain their leaves in winter, the tupelo
  has no need. A breeze comes. The morning

exhales the breath it's held, and a long,
  boat-shaped leaf falls at my feet to bleed.

◊◊◊

Under the cold souls of three pines, the house
  waits in limbo. Night composes its own stillness—

as if the floors and the kitchen table and chairs,
the bed and the oak cupboards and the teacups

and plates lie beneath a thick white web in a slow
  slumber of snow. Soon they will be invisible.

Deep inside the house, snow turns the dark
windows bright. From the sedge and peat pelt

of the hanging swamp beyond the fence, long blue
  feathers of shadow blow in across the thresh-

old. Like weary travellers they come, bearing
a message: everything that takes place here

in this house happens in its season. Outside,
    a plover calls in flight. A petal falls like a pale

    star across margins of space. Clouds drink
the moon and the world's gone in an instant.

Tonight, even the white poetry of the sky can't
    make its peace with what the snow knows.

◊◊◊◊

In the garden below the house,
    it's grown so high
these thirty years you've been here,
    from the crown
you can see Mount Cloudmaker
    through serrated leaves,

\*

lime-green in spring, then yellow,
    yellow. By wind,
it's travelled widely: her winged
    samara flies farther
than other seeds. And by sea—
    the long and straight

\*

wych elm trunks bend well, the per-
    fect steam-bent timber
for keels on boats, and barge hulls,
    and longbows
and coffin wood. In the shade
    of foliage so cool

*

and quiet, the golden elm makes
    safe your passage through
the underworld. Where you lie
    near the pond lined
with stone at the foot of the tree's
    clean bole in the shape

*

of a moon jar—an urn to hold
    the night—the tree's
breath is deeper than your own
    and when a shawl
of rain loosens, you taste the moist
    dirt, ash and mulch,

*

and map the lines on papery palms.
    Koi swim in and out
your open mouth. Purring gang-
    gangs lift their cloud-
grey wings. You are the falling leaf
    and the leaf fallen

*

and tendrils of your hair grow
    in rhizomes through
the earth. Your bones soften into
    branches, and on your
limbs, bright buds leap into light—
    leaf by golden leaf.

# 8mm

## Joe Dolce

When my father died, it fell to me
to clean his Fairport Harbor Ohio condo,
to box up belongings of two lives;
his, lost recently, and my mother's,
taken years earlier, but still
whispering in empty rooms,
fabrics and fragrances of furniture,
photo albums, lace fashioned
to protect arm rests, left in place,
after she left him to fold
her clothes, cook, sleep alone,
in their ghostly bed, and awaken
each morning to unfamiliar silence
and memories of missing touch,
from lives together for forever years.

The boxes were delivered flat.
I slotted them into squares,
visualizing arrangement of remnants
into cardboard, what to keep,
what to discard.
The bedroom had been the hardest
to desecrate, the underwear
and socks drawer, discovering,
beneath old newspaper liner,
three one-hundred dollar notes.
In the hall closet, where war rifles rested,
were ten boxes of ammunition
and a single roll of 8mm.

My father carried his Kodak slide camera
everywhere, in its small brown leather case,
to the Ardennes, to Normandy, to Korea,
imprinting glimpses of strange
and wonderful lands
and horrible times.
Home from service, slide nights
were usual family entertainment,
a cone of magic light, full of dust,
exciting the wall, Dad narrating.
I was allowed to stack
the little cardboard windows,
each a single film-frame,
in round carousels,
his remote ratcheting them
with military precision.

The 8mm was an anomaly
no one knew existed.
Projector gone, just a single reel,
in a time-weathered box.

I divided up the found money,
and money from sold guns, with siblings,
but kept the secret 8mm to myself.
I boxed up possessions,
some went to the tip, others to the second-hand.
I said something for the church service,
ate Italian food at the reception,
and stood quietly for his burial,
while a soldier folded a flag.

Back in Melbourne, I unpacked
my suitcases, forgetting the film.
It was tucked there, under my own socks.
No one owned these kind of projectors anymore,
so I sent the fragile footage away to be digitalized.
The USB I got back fit into my wallet.
In my darkened bedroom, computer light
brought grandparents back, my mother
and father, an array of cousins,
in splendid Sunday attire, there
for my 1965 High School graduation.
Everyone kissed everyone full on the lips,
something now rarely done amongst relatives.

The unknown video technician
had inserted sound under the film—
evocative guitar, and Cat Stevens singing,
*Where Do the Children Play?*
Music of the seventies,
under a lost family from the sixties,
reanimated here, in the 21st Century,
restoring, in flickering forgotten childhood,
a father's luminous farewell letter.

# Fragments

Kerry Greer

## I. Safe Place

In the night, I dream of people walking the streets
with flashlights. A group working together.
Daylight comes, and they are asleep where
nobody will find them.

## II. Contingency

I say, *There is a security alarm.*
I say, *There is a child.*
I say, *There is a knife.*
But it's all out of order.
The first thing is the child.
The first thing is:
I know the limit is something I don't know.

## III. School Drop-Off

Some days, I can't drive home
without him.

## IV. Husband

I have a flashlight too, in this dream.
I'm alone. As long as I don't find him,
he's alive. As long as I sleep,
it's a dream.

## V. Small

His bedroom is next to the front door.
These are the steps to take in an emergency,
or if he is coughing, fever-bright:
Lift him, move him to my bedroom.
Turn out the lights. Listen to him breathing,
and beyond? Maybe something, maybe nothing.
Animal-still. Cat. Fox.     Wolf—

## VI. You

Would you say: *Leave,*
or would you say: *Please?*
In the dark, you don't know yourself.
There is a gap between the mirror and the bed
where you could hide your child.    You would whisper:
*Do not make a sound,*
your voice a line of fear cold as
the other side of the bed, the hall, the

front door.

## VII. The Last Thing

He's the first thing. He's the first thing.

## VIII. Bat

Daylight comes, and the nocturnal world folds
around its creatures. In the night,
I keep a flashlight near my hand because
I can't sleep because
I'm listening. In the day,

he finds the flashlight, flicks it—
off on off on maybe off—
who will know
until later? We rush along the road
to school, late again.
The dream is never long enough,
waking-falling onto the stage
through the velvet and the ropes
from the eaves into painful light.
The finite scapula, the crumpled silk of shock,
the stage lights now amber, now red, now—

## IX. Meditation

*Get up. There is nobody else.*
*Get up.*

## X. A Truth and Two Lies

There is a knife.
There is a security alarm.
I think I would say: *Please.*

## XI. Please

*Please* at the corners of the mouth
like wings, triangles of black.
I know what the child would try to do
with the knife, near any man
who came near me.

## XII. Cut

fruit for breakfast, cut bread
along the bias, cut the crusts, cut packets
so he can open them at school, cut the talking,
cut the driving-time by one minute, cut the corners
off the road with the wheels of the car, the tyres marked by
isosceles—
indentations where someone lay soft in sleep against your
arm, the pressure of their collared pyjama—
shirt on the rubber of your skin.

## XIII. Either/Or

                                        Two things
The boy and his dead father.
The wolf and the knife.

                                        that will not meet.

## XIV. The Highest Shelf

To keep him safe.
Where I would never reach it in time.

## XV. Dream

In the safe place, there is a flashlight
and a boy bright as a knife
hidden by my side.

# D.I.Y. Eulogy

Mark O'Flynn

I am lost between the hammers and the wood chisels.
Light falls like talcum powder from the rafters
into the valleys between the hardware shelves. Awls
or owls? No, eels, yes, eels sway in the seaweed gloom.

Prevaricate a while. Leave those uncomfortable decisions
for the handy-persons of the congregation.
The one with the saw, the one with the pliers.
Priest. Dentist. Vivisectionist. Do your worst.

Dig a hole. With your spade make the sides perpendicular.
Get in. Lie down. Gaze up at the sky. The mourners,
backed by a screensaver of blue, cheer. Close your eyes
as, first the flowers, then the nails tumble down.

Papa. Reassemble your ash. Climb out of that box.
It's not time yet. Your chair is gathering lichen,
the screw-drivers chant your name.
None of your sentences have full stops.

Stop. After all that debt the beasts of the field still
own more of it than me. The grave has no
currency unless you are newly risen from it,
the paddocks filled with the perfidy of hope.

Go go go. Don't let the red light stop you. Disobey
those old imperatives. Stiffen the resolve of the up-
yours-finger as the motorcycle cop in his lunar
helmet pulls alongside you at the lights.

Fill the car with petrol. Turn off your mobile phone.
Not paying for fuel is a crime. Drive away slowly
as the moon follows you between the trees
writing everything down in its notebook.

It's an easy equation. Here a wicker basket with a
ribbon around its handle. Over there are your Red-
Riding Hood eggs. An aberrant stone, a tree root
on the path. Accident waiting to happen.

How could it be otherwise? Those clothes on the line
applauding the wind. The sight of fresh laundry,
or is it the smell, or rather the song? Clean cuffs
lifted up in praise, then disappointment, praise again.

My foot. My knee. My elbow. My lips. My love.
All stitched together with a dragonfly
into a semblance of this human form,
its silhouette enough to startle angels.

Relax. Put one foot in front of the other. Gather
a little speed. Lean forward to the runway. Faster now.
Feel the ground fall away. One wing beat at a time,
up up, as the air tells its tale.

Patience. All will be made clear in the end.
The confusion at the water hole as the predator
crawls on her belly through the grass. The bee-line
for nothing. The hammock will soon stop dripping.

Watch that river retract back up over the falls.
The rainbows all inverted, struggling to find a foothold
rocking on their backs like beetles in the wet air,
tadpoles reverting to their galaxy of spawn.

See the flight of blossom cascading
from one side of the street to the other. In the vortex
between the vertical and horizontal things
could be worse, immeasurable, endless.

Ignore the sunlight photosynthesising all those leaves.
The dappled shadows will a pretty picture make,
like shillings of light floating on the sun-stained water.
Come back to bed. Put your lips to sleep on mine.

Press your mouth against my throat and hum.
There is sweet music to be made in this factory.
The bees in my gullet making all that honey.
The slugs making all that jam. Take these ants

for instance, industrious and uncomplaining, going
about their thankless work as if the creator has parted
the clouds and is about to pass down judgment
on each and every one,

his disembodied voice like a fog horn, his wrath
like hail. The process is simple. Stop denigrating
the house of your ancestors, (the trees, the earth).
Allow it another breath

as the building sighs to its timbers.
Together we'll mourn our neglect.
Every Saturday afternoon as we prepare
our threnody, the kilns smoke in the cellar.

# Habitat for Humans

SJ Finn

It's drizzling when I arrive. I double listen, know what to expect: *Coppin Centre Reception … Here for a visit.* I'm short talking because a journalist is reading her piece about the prison at Guantanamo Bay. *The place, she says, has its own justice system: no charges, no trials, just lots of torture.* The door hums, makes a note—C major with a dash of bass, Lou Reed swinging through an

introduction. The mechanics gather, node to root path, a click of the door's tongue, an invitation dubiously given: Hotel California, Ravenhall Correctional, a passage through the Kármán line. I grapple with my protection. There are straps that go all the way around my headphones. The moment flattens, gravity eases. I think about entropy declining into order, the natural undoing of

cellular automaton, arrays of tessellation trapped in a box for a beat, reality suspended, memory gone. *Suspects are disappeared into a netherworld of black sites.* The second door repeats the hum and release. I step from void to vicissitudes, eyes on the visitors upright in chairs. One man has his wiry-haired dog at his feet. I quick grin him. *Water-boarding and force-feeding, sleep and sensory* deprivation; something called walling. *A man dies of hypothermia, left on a concrete floor. Another has injuries from arms tied high and feet tied low.* On the monitor my face marries a smiley emoji. The gadget beeps, tells me I'm too cold. I remove my dark glasses hoping that will assist. *You've been outside.* The receptionist is smiling. I'm double listening again. *Your skin,* she says. *Winter in the south.* Or

I think those are her words. I nod regardless, pick up a test kit, secret it into my pocket. At home I've built a Jenga tower of the plastic sleeve results. Upstairs, I pass the nurses' station, then Mitch's room, then Marg's then Michael's then Buffy's then June's. Through my mother's doorway, sitting by her big window, her head bobs as if there's a short in her wiring. She greets me in her now-tone of gratitude and softness. She should, she says, be gone. We discuss Edna, the woman who lived in the room further along the hallway and who died last week. *She looked like Dad before he went,* I tell Mum. *Do I look like that?* she asks, her brow raised in youthful faith. *No,* I laugh. *You're not even close.* She tells me about her Aunt Bessie, whose hands were full of groceries (*Did people have string bags back then?*) when the neighbours' goat ran at her and wrapped its tether around her legs. She fell and broke a tooth. Our gaze shifts. In the corridor, a woman moves at glacial pace. Others follow. I think about agility: a marker in the galaxy of brutal beginnings and endings. *There they go,* my mother says. We watch the bent shuffling parade pass her door. *There were plane loads of orange-suited men, shackled at the ankles and blind-folded by gaffer-taped goggles, being led to outdoor wire-mesh cages.* We talk about the traffic and the leafless tree, outside. Is it a maple? The tea cart rattles. We both have milk in our coffee but neither of us eat the cake which comes without a question. Clean towels & laundry-in-a-long-blue-bag like all residents get. I put Mum's clothes onto hangers and prepare to repeat my entrance

in reverse. Head-phones constitute a diorama as if what I hear I see. Reminds me of the black matter scientists say is in me, rushing like a wind. The journalist quotes a man whose son died in the Bali bombings. *I don't believe in a system that locks people up without a trial.* The foyer is empty. I nod to the woman at reception. She flips a lever behind the desk. The first door opens. I remove my protection.

*Acknowledgement: The essay mentioned in this poem is *The Trial* by Bronwyn Adcock. The italics are not direct quotes.

# Social distance
### Rachael Mead

1. #couchlyf

The Great Storm of 2020 rolled out indoors.
Before now, news seemed careless.
We could take it or leave it. On TV
I see people go to bars, catch elevators,
kiss. It's so casual. *Twelfth floor, please.*
*See you.* And I feel as if I'm watching
something decadent from a golden age—
Scott & Zelda splashing through fountains
drunk and glittering. I took it for granted.
The full supermarket shelves. The freedom to jump
in the car on a whim. Go to work.
Hug my friends. Rub my eyes without
thinking of respirators, hand sanitiser
and the collapse of global markets.

Anxiety roils like my last pot of ramen
but the bad weather is all in my head.
The sky is a clean blue bowl. We drink beer,
drag the couch outside and watch the waves
fling themselves on the granites in either
grief or joy. It's just one more uncertainty.
I call Mum, her voice enfolded in smoke.
No veggie seedlings at the garden centre.
Dad's grumpy. No, she doesn't need anything.
*It's just good to hear your voice.* We watch
the syrup of sunset thicken, then head inside
to curl up in last week's unmade bed, lips
stumbling to mouth words we have yet to invent
as we try to teach ourselves new ways to pray.

## 2. Zeno's Paradox in lockdown

Through the honeyed slide of hours
I practice the art of arrangement,
composing the room into this day's
still life. The books. The lamps.
The empty vase, just so. The treacled
gradient of light and cool subtraction
of dusk. Time sliced so thin it stops.

They say binaries are dead. Perhaps
that's true, in everything but code.
Yet here I sit, trapped between
life and death, every viscous instant
sliding slow as Zeno's Paradox, waiting
for all the infinite divisions between
one and zero to clot into days.

The window tenderly cups its garden.
This poem, even in all its black and
white weightlessness, is at heart
just one more still life unsure of its true
nature—particle or wave or some
unknown in-between—as I inch along
this immeasurable path towards zero.

## 3. The death of walking

Last year in that boot-shaped land, life was all about feet.
Size eleven, bunions, footprints like continents. The delight
of strolling from the sun-strewn Spanish Steps to the alleys
of Aventino, my stride threaded with stress after scattering
self-respect in the gutter outside the Baths of Caracalla.

Trundling my suitcase to the foot of the Alps, at last and again
it was all about feet. Everyday sunshine and grasslands boiling
with colour and cowbells. At home, to walk alone was an act

of greed. There, I swung my arms, free of guilt and leash and
strode those hills, my limp sounding the valleys to a solo beat.

Today, these ugg boots whiff of wet fur but the couch is bare.
My heart slugs indigo inside my ribs. Time is thinner here.
A place where even soft things break. There's no reason to walk.
The pace of my days no longer thumps to tailbeat or wet-nosed
pleas for scent-snuffle or messages left on bark. The leash hangs
by the door. The outside is a fable I once believed. Days pass
coated in burrs. Boots gather dust and the fruit bowl grows fur.
Weak light slides in but the beds of sun lie empty. This ache
is fractal, hollowness blooming boundless hollows, ears tuned
for the jingle of tags that does not come. World-worn, I tuck
away my feet. The empty couch stretches itself, quiet and cold.

4. Self-portrait reflected in the TV

The first thing you'll notice is hair.
The kitchen looms like Satan
in the background. Silver shapes
curl beside me. A wolf and a greyhound.
A kelpie, a ridgeback, a tortoiseshell cat.
One living, four ghosts. It's dark as childhood,
hermetic as a ship trapped in a bottle.
You can't tell my jacket is blood-red
in the screen's liquid black.

There are books. Pens. A vase of beauty
some call weeds. Reading glasses
with a crooked right arm. Puppy-chewed,
a detail mentioned in the interpretive panel.
If you knew me, you'd be surprised
the tv is off, expecting my reflection
as a double exposure across *Black Widow*
or a Wes Anderson film. The notebook is open.
The light in the room is blue wren song,
the soundtrack a podcast by Natalie Haynes.

Dim as an engine room at night
the room's vibrancy is a secret.
Even my face is grey-scale.
This is no Nerudan 'Self-portrait as an
animal of light'. Ideally, there'd be
symbolism artfully strewn about.
A few *memento mori*. A globe.
A skull. Significantly selected titles.
Instead, there's my diary and a 'to do' list.
There *is* a stuffed raven. On the walls,
forgeries. Rivera. Kahlo. Preston.
You can't see the Van Gogh. You can't
see the construction, stroke by stroke,
of something that doesn't say anything new.
The whole idea is to instil doubt.
Is this an original? A forgery? A copy of a forgery?
In the dark mirror, the spectre shifts,
crossing her legs. Her pen scrawls across the page.
But you can't read the words.

5. The Lady of Shalott in 2020

The grand architecture of the world
has shrunk to my fence-line
and places I love call out in thin voices
as if locked in distant rooms.

My days unspool in a single stretch
of light, stained only by the ordinary
miracles of cloud track, voice mote
and the thump and drag of blood.

My mind is the bathroom mirror
after a shower. It's not death or curse
or loneliness I fear. It's forgetting who I am.
A woman in love with the wild.

Each day I knot words onto pages, trace
the path of the planet by the cedar's shadow,
study the syntax of birds. Curling toes in the grass,
I dream the history of this place layering down

to its dark core—molten and churning.
In the old world, enchanted by light and quiet,
I was not in love with people. Yet here I am, half-sick
of shadows. The night rides in. The stars hang,

keeping their distance. I gaze out at the world
through the glass but see nothing. No passing knight.
No bearded meteor. No broad stream complaining
in its banks. Just my reflection crack'd from side to side.

Note: 'half-sick of shadows', 'passing knight', 'bearded meteor', 'broad stream complaining'
and 'crack'd from side to side' are references to the poem 'The Lady of Shalott' by Alfred Lord
Tennyson 1832.

# Fall

## Mark Tredinnick

*What anchors us*
*    to this thirst*
*& earth, its threats*

*& thinnesses—*
*    its ways of waning*
*& making the most of—*

*of worse & much*
*    worse—if not*
*this light lifting*

*up over the ridge*

—Kevin Young, 'Ledge'


IF SIX thousand small craft
      Put out to sea in failing light,
  Each lit by its single lamp, and

If these were the barques
    Of the dead—

Interceded for by all the light
    Of a long dry autumn
Staunched now in winter's first cold front—

And if these boats, coracles, say, were headed
    Back toward the living shores,
Redeemed, they might turn out to be
    This very moment when I drive around
The corner and into this epiphany: the elm, a hundred

Summers in, its leaves a yellow fleet,
    The rain, an open sea.

***

I don't think I ever saw
        A fall so full, or trees
In their failing arcades pull

Such a festival down
        From the sky as this year

I did. And I am supposed to be
        A poet, so I will not speak
In primary tones; I will say instead:

Saffron, aubergine,
        Scarlet, terra cotta. The vivid battalions

Of immigrant trees.

But for the tenor of the leaves of the elm
        At the corner, there is only the tone a painter
Might choose for canola fields in flower—

The colour of the better angels of loss's second self.
        And there is only the rain,

In which that intonation runs.

***

I never ran a light so red
        As the way the end of day billowed
About two maple saplings in the street

Last week before the rain. Who knew trees
        Could so irradiate a dusk?

Or how little two dogs could care
        When I pulled their running short to shoot
A moment as revolutionary as the death

Of a regime. So does the world convince you
        Again with its forms, its plays of light.

Who knew the end could come
        So sweetly, that passing could so still you
In your tracks?

\*\*\*

Loss is the plot you walk
        From the womb. You're on your way

To ceasing from the start. Life is a story
        That never ends well, no matter
How well it went. Land is longer. Music. Sometimes

Love. Let's do those. Be letters, pinoak leaves,
        Fetlocks, phrases, raised arms, river bends,

Bird cadences, old limbs, clouds. Escarpments.
        Two trees at dawn. The way the shade
Forgives the sun. The insurgency of a harvest

Moon. First snow. These may be the faith you keep
        With life, all dying notwithstanding.
They—and now this

Space between a heartbeat and a thought
        And the landing of the finger on the key—

These are how the dead go on
        In us, and love makes do in loss, like leaves
In rain. These moments of a mind

Without an end. This unceasing ceasing
       That is life's precondition for living
On. The broken heart of time.

These are the rules for paradise,
       Moonlighting among us in the long shade of the fall.

\*\*\*

And I should be thinking
       Of the season and how the body, wasting,

Wastes so fine, and how the mind, weathering,
       Becomes the mirror image of the soul. And the heart
Lets go of summers that long ago let go

Of the heart. I should be,
       Like Rexroth one autumn

In California, *calling the stiff mind*
       Again to *passion*, but I watch the sky
Contuse over Khartoum, azure

As any afternoon in autumn
       Over the Wingecarribee,

A violent desert pastoral, and my mind, out walking dogs,
       Finds it hard to breathe
Interred down deep in the fallen stories

Of a Turkish town, and fire bombs
       Flay Odessa, and the sea ice fails the sea,

       And a whole hemisphere burns,

And two-hundred-and thirty years
       Of adverse possession
Still seem like too little time to shame

My fellow countrymen
    Into shutting for one moment

The flying fuck up
    And listening to the lives their own
Ill-gotten being here has unhoused.

It is the anniversary or a mother's death
    And I can't help wishing she'd

Been licensed this one last fall,
    This sacrament, this haloed send off.

                    \*\*\*

Beauty breaks out, like panic, among the worthy
    And the undeserving, without discrimination,
Defying all that theory had so earnestly

Foretold. God, worn with the waiting,
    Has fallen from the last known purgatorial perch

On earth, *but see how her saints still burn*
    The dying season onto your retina, as you turn
The wheel and put out from port

    And make for poor Ithaka again.

# About The Poets

### Eileen Chong

Eileen Chong is a poet of Hakka, Hokkien, and Peranakan descent. She is the author of nine books. Her work has shortlisted for numerous awards, including twice for the Prime Minister's Literary Award. Her next poetry collection, *We Speak of Flowers*, is forthcoming with UQP in 2025. She lives and works on the unceded lands of the Gadigal people.

### Joe Dolce

2021 City of Melbourne Poet Laureate. Highly Commended 2020 ACU Poetry Prize. Short List 2020 & 2014 Newcastle Poetry Prize. Shortlist 2019, 2018, 2017 & 2014 University of Canberra Vice-Chancellor's Poetry Prize. Winner of 2017 University of Canberra Health Poetry Prize. Best Australian Poems 2015 & 2014. Winner of 25th Launceston Poetry Cup. Recipient of Advance Australia Award. *www.atthenoisycafe.com*

### SJ Finn

SJ Finn (she/her) is from Melbourne, Australia. Longlisted for the Peter Porter prize and shortlisted for the Val Vallis Award, she won the Emerging Poet's Award from Queensland Poetry. Her work has appeared in the Griffith Review, Overland, The Age newspaper, Cordite and Rabbit. She can be found at: *www.sjfinn.com*

### Jo Gardiner

Jo Gardiner's novel, *The Concerto Inn*, was published by UWA Press in 2006. Most recently she was shortlisted for the 2023 Gwen Harwood Poetry Prize and the ACU Poetry Prize, as well as the 2022 *Island* Nonfiction Prize. She was a finalist in the 2022 Montreal International Poetry Prize.

### Susan Garman

Susan Garman's first book of poetry, *Of rain and other things*, was published by Ginninderra Press in 2022. She grew up in Melbourne and lives in Canberra.

### Jake Goetz

Jake Goetz has published two collections of poetry, *meditations with passing water* (Rabbit, 2018), which was shortlisted for the Queensland Premier's Award, and *Unplanned Encounters: Poems 2015-2020* (Apothecary Archive, 2023). He is a DCA candidate at the Writing & Society Research Centre and the Reviews Editor at *Plumwood Mountain*.

## Kerry Greer

Kerry Greer is an award-winning poet and writer based in Western Australia. She received the Venie Holmgren Prize for Environmental Poetry in 2021. Her work is widely published in journals and anthologies. As a widow and solo parent, Kerry has a particular interest in writing about grief and what comes after loss. Her debut poetry collection will be published by Recent Work Press in November 2023.

## Andrew Heath

A writer and visual artist, Andrew 's poetry has been published in journals including two previous NPP anthologies, Weekend Australian, Westerly, Vernacular, Geek Mook, Rush and Hope. A Mental Health Social Worker working in Karratha on Ngarluma country, Andrew shares four children and four grandchildren with his wife Julie.

## Paul Hetherington

Paul Hetherington has published 17 collections of poetry, including *Ragged Disclosures* (2022) and *Her One Hundred and Seven Words* (2021). With Cassandra Atherton, he co-authored *Prose Poetry: An Introduction* (Princeton UP, 2020) and co-edited the *Anthology of Australian Prose Poetry* (Melbourne UP, 2020). He is co-editor of *Axon: Creative Explorations*.

## Christopher (Kit) Kelen

Kit Kelen has published more than a dozen volumes of poetry in English over the last thirty years, as well as books of poetry in a dozen languages other than English. Kelen's latest English language poetry volume is *Book of Mother* (Puncher & Wattmann, 2022).

## Jean Kent

Jean Kent lives at Lake Macquarie, NSW. Nine books of her poetry have been published. The most recent is *The Shadow Box* (Pitt Street Poetry, 2023). Her next book, combining poems about Paris with paintings by her husband Martin, is forthcoming from Pitt Street Poetry early in 2024.

## Jennifer Kornberger

Jennifer Kornberger is a poet and creator of performance events. Her first collection of poetry *I could be rain* was published by Sunline Press. She is a past winner of the Tom Collins Prize and has received commendations in the Newcastle Poetry Prize. She is co-director of *www.theatreofthesea.net*

## Roberta Lowing

Roberta Lowing's poetry collections include *Ruin*, a 55-poem sequence in four voices on the Iraq War; *The Searchers*; and, most recently, the environmental collection *This Attic Of Fire* (Apothecary Archive Press). Roberta's first novel, *Notorious*, was shortlisted for the Prime Minister's Literary Awards and the Commonwealth Book Prize.

## Rachael Mead

Rachael Mead is a South Australian novelist and poet. She's the author of the novel *The Application of Pressure* (Affirm Press 2020) and four collections of poetry including *The Flaw in the Pattern* (UWAP 2018). Her second novel *The Art of Breaking Ice* was published in July this year.

## Audrey Molloy

Audrey Molloy grew up in Ireland and has lived in Sydney since 1998. Her poetry collections include, *The Important Things* (The Gallery Press, 2021), which received the Anne Elder Award, *Ordinary Time* (Pitt Street Poetry, 2022), a collaboration with Australian poet Anthony Lawrence, and *The Blue Cocktail* (The Gallery Press / Pitt Street Poetry, 2023).

## Mark O'Flynn

Mark O'Flynn's novel *The Last Days of Ava Langdon* (UQP) was short listed for the Miles Franklin Award, 2017. A collection of short stories *Dental Tourism* appeared in 2020. His recent collections of poems are *Undercoat* (Liquid Amber Press, 2022), and *Einstein's Brain* (Puncher & Wattmann, 2022).

## Vuong Pham

Vuong Pham is an Asian-Australian poet & modern haiku advocate. You can read more of his work at: *vuongphampoetry.wordpress.com*

## Bronwyn Rodden

Bronwyn is an award-winning artist and writer. Following an MA Writing (UTS), she was selected for *Scarp/UW New Poets Program*, awarded an Australia Council *Emerging Writer Grant* and a *Bundanon Fellowship*. She is published in literary journals and anthologies, including the recent *International Anthology of Surrealist and Magic Realist Poetry*.

## Robyn Rowland

Robyn Rowland has 14 books, 11 poetry, including *Under This Saffron Sun—Safran Güneşin Altında*, Turkish translations, Mehmet Ali Çelikel, (Ireland, 2019). Her poetry appears in national/international journals, over forty anthologies, eight editions of *Best Australian Poems*. Her readings for *National Irish Poetry Reading Archive,* James Joyce Library, UCD, available on *YouTube*.

## Craig Smith

Craig is a special education teacher and researcher. He has presented globally on neurodiversity and emerging technologies, including workshops for the United Nations. Outside of education, he is a pipe organist and published composer of experimental music works. Craig lives in Newcastle with his wife, daughter, son and Finnish Lapphund.

## Kevin Smith

Kevin's worked as teacher, writer, actor, and workshop facilitator. Two collections of his poetry have been published: *Awake to the Rest of My Days* (2021) and *Another Day* (2023). His poems are often anthologised. In 2022, he placed 2nd in The ACU, and shortlisted in The Newcastle, and The Bridport.

## Mark Tredinnick

Mark Tredinnick is a celebrated Australian poet whose honours include two Newcastle Poetry Prizes, the Montreal and the Blake. *A Beginner's Guide* (2022) and *House of Thieves* (2023) are his latest books. *Nine Carols* comes out in November.

## Todd Turner

Todd Turner is an Australian poet, and goldsmith. His first two collections of poetry are *Woodsmoke* (Black Pepper Publishing) and *Thorn* (Puncher and Wattmann). His poems have been widely published. He is currently working on a manuscript for his third collection.

## Dženana Vucic

Dženana Vucic is a Bosnian-Australian writer, poet and critic. She is currently working on a book about the Bosnian war, identity, memory and un/belonging. Her writing has appeared in *Sydney Review of Books, Cordite, Overland, Meanjin, Kill Your Darlings, Australian Poetry Journal,* and others. She tweets at @dzenanabanana.

## Jo Ward

Jo Ward is an emerging Australian writer living in Kupidabin, Queensland. Her poems have recently appeared in the *Australian Poetry Anthology* and *Griffith Review*. She is the author of *A Quiet Sorcery* (Hardie Grant, 2022), a collaborative book of visual poetry informed by her experience living with cervical dystonia.

www.ingramcontent.com/pod-product-compliance
Lightning Source LLC
Chambersburg PA
CBHW030411120726
47904CB00007B/2231